For
Now

CHELSEA M. CAMERON

Chapter One

'm used to having my ass grabbed. Hell, some nights it feels like I've got bruises. But tonight I'm not in the mood. I haven't had sex in a long time, I've got PMS and I'm not in the mood for guys who think my ass belongs to them. So when one of my cheeks gets pinched as I bring a tray of drinks to a table, I lose it.

"You do that again and those fingers are going to be gone," I say, grabbing the guy's hand and pulling his thumb toward his wrist. The guy yelps and tries to get free.

"What the fuck, bitch?!" His buddies just laugh and make jokes about me being a handful in the bedroom. I can see their rings glinting in the smoky light. I'm sure they make wonderful husbands.

I toss my dark hair over my shoulder. "My ass is not your property. My ass belongs to me and I decide who touches it, got it?" I stare down into the guy's face as it goes redder and redder.

He swears at me some more and then I let him go, flinging his arm back so he loses his drunken balance and tips over onto the floor. I leave a smattering of applause in my wake as I head back to the bar.

"Now if I told you that turned me on, would I get the same treatment?" a voice says behind me as I hop over the bar.

I spin around and roll my eyes. Javier. Of course.

He just grins at me and my stomach does little flips. Javi is attractive and he knows it. Once upon a time, when I'd first met him, I would have jumped right into bed with him. He has all the right stuff in all the right places. I don't even need to see him naked to know that. But things are complicated and now it doesn't seem like a good idea. Besides, he yelled at me for being a crappy friend to Shannon and I'm still a little sore about it. Had I been a crappy friend? Yup. But I didn't need him telling me that.

"I wouldn't touch you with a ten-foot-pole," I say, fixing him with my best withering stare.

He wiggles his eyebrows but I won't let my focus be drawn to his eyes. They're this dark brown color, with little bits of almost gold. Not that I've paid much attention to them or anything.

"I've got a pole for you, gorgeous. It's not ten feet but…" I make a disgusted sound, but honestly? The thought of Javier's "pole" gets me all hot and bothered.

The guy is seriously jacked. Plus, his arms are covered in dark sexy tats. I really have to stop looking at his arms.

"You're disgusting," I say, narrowing my eyes. "And I'm busy. Go find someone else to annoy with your presence."

"You adore me, gorgeous. Plus, I'm not grabbing your ass like those dipshits over there." He jerks his thumb toward the table with the guys I'd just left. They're laughing loudly and drunkenly and making a nuisance of themselves. But what else is new? This is a bar after all, where drinking is encouraged.

"I'm busy," I say, heading toward the other end of the bar where a girl waves me down for another Sex on the Beach. Javier follows me and waits, leaning his huge arms on the sticky bar. I try not to think of those arms hoisting me off my feet and holding me against his hard body.

I get the girl her drink and then serve a few more, including a row of shots. To be fancy, I flip the shot glasses up and catch them before

I pour. When I first got this job I practiced for ages with plastic cups in my apartment and Shannon as my only audience. I figured having fancy serving skills might earn me extra tips and I need all the tips I can get to pay for law school.

"So, when are you done?" Javier says when there's a lull in the action. I fiddle around with the cash register, pretending I'm still busy.

"Never," I say. I'm going to resist him, I am.

"Oh, come on. You know you want to hang out with me. I know Jett is at your place getting busy with Shannon and my bed is nice and big and empty. Well, except for me, but there's plenty of room." I try to halt the images of just what we could get accomplished in his big bed and fail.

Must. Resist. Javier.

He might have been easier to resist if his name wasn't so sexy. And his arms weren't so nice. And his eyes didn't look at me like he wanted to taste every inch of me.

"Go away, Javier." Saying his name turns me on. This is a serious problem. "What are you doing here? Don't you have other, easier, girls to pester?"

He laughs and leans closer, looking right and left.

"I don't want easy. I like a challenge. And you, Hazel Gellar, are my kind of challenge." Before I can say or do anything, he hauls himself up on the bar and plants a kiss on my lips.

I'm too shocked to move so I just stare at him.

"See you later, gorgeous." And with a wink, he's gone.

I lick my lips and try not to think about how much I like the taste of Javier.

At three in the morning, I creep back into the apartment as quietly as I can. But as I walk past Shannon's room, I can hear her voice and Jett's, talking low. They're in the honeymoon part of their relationship, so they spend most of their time talking, having sex, or talking about having sex. I'm not jealous or anything, I swear.

I head right for the shower and peel off my slutty bartender outfit. Disgusting as it may be, dressing sexy earns me more tips. After washing off the night, I go right to bed, not even bothering to put anything on. The nights are still cool, but I like the feel of my sheets on my skin after a shower. It's one of life's simple pleasures.

I set the alarm on my phone and fall into an exhausted sleep.

Unfortunately, the lovebirds in the kitchen wake me only a few hours later. I'm so, so, so happy for Shannon and Jett is a great guy, but being around them when they're all couple-y and cutesy is hard to take sometimes.

Then I hear a third voice that I don't expect. So I put on a baggy sweatshirt and shorts and stumble into the kitchen to find Javi pouring batter into the waffle iron while Jett and Shannon sit stuffing their faces at the table. And Shannon has that horrible bear mug out that she got on her date with Jett a few weeks ago.

"What did I tell you about that mug?" I say, and they all freeze and stare at me.

"What are you doing up?" Shannon says, moving the mug behind a stack of mail. I know it's there, so her moving it does absolutely no good. I have a thing against objects being shaped like living creatures. It's not natural. I can feel it staring at me and plotting to kill me in my sleep with its little ceramic bear paws.

"The three of you were loud," I say, glaring at Javier, who's whistling and looking fresh and clean and even more edible than the waffles he's piled on a plate.

"Aw, I'm sorry. You usually sleep right through everything," Shannon says, brushing her blonde hair out of her big blue eyes. She's one of those girls who looks so innocent, she could basically get away with anything.

"Yeah, well, I guess I just couldn't last night." I can't be too much of a bitch to her. I'm still trying to make up for all the other times I've been a bitch to her, including driving her to fake a relationship (which turned out okay in the end anyway) just so I'd stop pestering her about losing her virginity. I'm going to be making up for that one for a very long time.

"You know what'll make it better? Waffles." Javier shoves a plate in my face, and my stomach rumbles. Normally I'm not hungry in the morning, but these aren't just any waffles. These are made-by-Javier waffles. I've eaten his food before (not a euphemism) and he's an amazing cook. Like, should-have-his-own-show-on-the-Food-Network good.

"Sleep. Sleep would make it better," I say, falling into the only other chair we have in our kitchen. "I need a cigarette." That will make it better. Cigarette before waffles.

Shannon makes a face, but I tell her I'll go outside. I grab my smokes and a lighter and head out to stand on the steps. The door opens behind me and I'm joined by Javier.

"Aren't you supposed to be watching the waffles?" I say, shielding the cigarette from the wind so I can light it.

"Jett has temporary custody. Got one for me?" I hold the pack out and he takes one, putting it in his mouth and then leaning toward me so I'll light it for him. Once again, I roll my eyes, but he just winks at me and then inhales, his eyes closing in ecstasy.

"Fuck, I missed that. I've been trying to quit," he says, blowing the smoke away from me.

"Yeah, me too. I'm only a stress smoker really. Or a social smoker." Yup, this is definitely making me feel better. It's not just the nicotine, it's the act of smoking that calms my nerves.

"Jett quit cold turkey, the bastard."

"Shannon never started. But she's a much better person than I am." In so many ways.

"Being good is all right for some people, but a little bit of bad can go a long way." Javier is one of those people who makes everything, and I mean EVERYTHING, into an innuendo. He just can't help himself.

We finish our smokes in silence and then wait for a few minutes to go back inside. Summer is coming, but Spring still has us in its somewhat chilly grip. I pull the hood on my sweatshirt up, but Javi is completely comfortable in just a t-shirt. Those damn arms must keep him pretty warm. They'd definitely keep me plenty warm.

God, I have to stop thinking of him in sexual terms.

"Thanks for the smoke," he says before opening the door and going back inside. I wait for another few seconds before I follow him.

Chapter Two

I'm a grump the rest of the day, due to my lack of sleep. Or at least I'm going to blame it on that. And it only gets worse, with the morons in my classes being at their most moronic. I mean, seriously, how hard is it to read a chapter in a textbook and then discuss the stuff you read? Hell, I don't have a photographic memory or anything, but I'm at least able to do that.

None of these people will hack it in law school. I honestly can't wait until all I have to do is read law books and do mock trials. It makes me tingly just thinking about it.

I knew I wanted to be a lawyer before I even knew what a lawyer did. I have the proof from first grade when we all listed what we wanted to be. Most kids picked President or astronaut or even a unicorn, but I explained to my teacher what I wanted to do (my parents had been watching *Law and Order*) and she told me that was a lawyer. And that's been my dream ever since. I think it's one of the reasons Shannon and I get along so well. We both have dreams that we've had for so long we don't remember not having them.

The girl in front of me in my Macroeconomics class falls asleep and I resist the urge to poke her with my pencil to wake her up. Even with my crazy hours, I've never fallen asleep in class. The energy shots I take might have something to do with that though.

Shannon's at work when I get back from my early evening class, so it's up to me to try to make dinner. I'm not a bad cook, I swear. I just… I'm not very good at it. I don't know why. Usually my meals are limited to stuff that comes in boxes and take less than three steps to prepare. And then some nights we eat cereal out of the box.

I'm just looking through the cabinets, trying to find something, anything, that appeals to me. Nothing does. And then there's a knock at the door.

Weird.

I go to answer it and find Javi, grinning at me with a bunch of grocery bags.

"What the hell are you doing here?" I say, crossing my arms. It's been a long day and I don't have the patience to deal with him.

"I'm making you dinner, gorgeous. Shannon is out with Jett, so I figured you might be eating alone and that would be a tragedy."

"You 'figured' I'd be eating alone? What the fuck, Javi?"

He at least has the decency to look a little sheepish.

"That didn't come out the way I wanted it to. Are you going to let me in?" I narrow my eyes, but my hunger wins out. If there's one thing Javi can do, other than annoy the crap out of me, it's cook.

He sets the bags down on the counter and starts pulling things out. I gotta be honest, I don't know what some of them are.

"Pots and pans?" he says, and I get them down from the top of the cabinet.

He makes a face.

"Teflon? Seriously? You don't have any cast iron?" I have no idea what he's talking about. A pan is a pan, right?

"Uh, no? What's the difference?" Now he gives me a look as if I've lost my damn mind.

"Shit, it's no wonder you can't cook." That comment earns him a smack, but his arm is so rock-hard with muscle, I'm the one who suffers. "Hey, no assaulting the chef. Unless it's, you know..." He wiggles his eyebrows and I want to strangle him. Why did I let him in? I don't think a good meal is worth this.

"Oh come on. I'll teach you. I know you're smarter than me. You just need the right teacher." This is the first thing he's ever said to me that doesn't sound sexual. I am shocked beyond belief.

"Fine. What are we making?" He has an awful lot of stuff for one dinner.

"Fettuccini with shrimp and red peppers in a cream sauce, balsamic Brussels sprouts and we'll do lemon bars for dessert." Shit, that all sounds good.

"You're going to teach me to make that? The girl who can screw up anything cooking-related?" I am very skeptical of this venture.

"Yup. If you can remember all that law shit I know you know, you can make this. Promise." He wasn't going to give up, so I sighed in defeat.

"Okay, where do we start?"

Cooking with Javi is different than I thought it would be. Honestly, I thought he was going to yell at me and make everything sexual and turn it into a shitty experience. But, who knew, he's actually a good teacher. Patient, and doesn't call me an idiot for asking questions. He even lets me stir and doesn't try to take over.

It's the most pleasant few hours I've ever had with him, and it makes me wonder if this is really him, or if he's just trying hard to not be his usual self.

"So is this what you do to impress all the girls? Cook for them?" I ask as he drains the pasta in the sink and then tosses it into the pot with the sauce, shrimp and peppers.

He laughs.

"Hell, no. But they don't want me to cook for them. That's not what they come to me for. Some things are about sex and nothing else." Wow, that's brutally honest.

"Don't you think you're using them?" I say, leaning against the counter as he stirs.

"Nope. Because we're both consenting adults and I don't give them anything they don't ask for and vice versa. If there's one thing I've learned, it's that women want casual sex even more than men sometimes. And I am happy to provide a service." There's the Javier I know.

"Aren't you just a regular philanthropist? They should give you a plaque." He laughs again and turns the burner down.

"I'm like Oprah. She gives out cars. I give out orgasms." My mouth drops open and then I start laughing.

"You get an orgasm and you get an orgasm. Everyone gets an orgasm!" I yell in my best Oprah impression. The two of us are laughing our asses off and I realize I'm having a good time with him. All the lost sleep and general life irritation is gone.

"What can I say? It's a gift," he says. "It would be wrong of me to not share my gift with as many ladies as possible." I can't argue with that ridiculous logic. Besides, I can't cast any stones because I've done the exact same thing.

"Pig," I say, throwing an oven mitt at him, which he catches. Of course.

We sit down and everything shifts. It feels so… domestic. Not like we're married or anything, but almost like we're a couple having dinner together like we do every night.

"So how was your day, dear?" Javi says, as if reading my mind.

"Crap. But it's getting better." I don't mean to be so honest, but it just comes out. Maybe Shannon is rubbing off on me.

"Same here. This guy in my graphic design class ended up deleting his entire project. Moron didn't save anything. You should have seen his face. I almost died." He chuckles to himself.

"Graphic design? What is your major anyway?" I realize I've never asked. But he knows my major and a whole lot of other things I don't remember ever telling him.

"I'm a double major in computer science and graphic design with minors in sociology and literature. And if you tell anyone that, I will be forced to kill you." Now THAT is cause for a jaw drop. Shit, that's a lot of classes. I had no idea.

I sputter as Javi twirls some pasta on his fork.

"See, this is why I don't tell people and let them just make their own assumptions," he says, staring at the pasta on his fork before putting it in his mouth. He's actually got great table manners. Yet another surprise.

"Shit. You're making me feel like an underachiever. How in the hell are you taking all those classes?" I ask.

He shrugs one shoulder. Yeah, right no big deal.

"There are 24 hours in a day. I can get a lot done in a short amount of time. And I don't sleep a lot." Clearly.

"So what are you going to do with all those degrees?"

He shrugs again. Javier isn't a fan of talking about himself. Noted.

"Not sure yet." I have to call bullshit on that. Anyone who's that serious about college and classes has a plan. He *has* to have some kind of plan.

"Really?"

He runs his hand through his hair. "Jesus, what is this, an interrogation? You going to water-board me next?"

Touchy, touchy. "No, I just realized I don't know much about you, you asshole. Don't blame a girl for trying to get to know you. I won't do it again." I stab a shrimp and picture Javier's head on the pale pink body.

"Why do you want to know? Why do you *care*?" He says "care" like it's a dirty word. I don't care. I mean, I care a little. He is my roommate's boyfriend's best friend. So a little care is involved. But I don't care *a lot*.

"Just curious. And I don't care. I don't care what you do or who you do it with." The easygoing banter we shared just a few minutes ago is gone and in its place is something more… hostile.

"Didn't think so," he says and goes back to his pasta and Brussels sprouts. I never thought I liked those things, but I'd eat them every day if Javi made them like this. They're freaking delicious.

We finish the rest of the meal in silence, except when Javi grabs the dishes from me, and silences my protests with a look.

"Oh, you'll do my dishes but not your own? Who cares now, Javi?" I know for a fact that he's a slob at his own place because Jett complains about it to Shannon and then Shannon complains to me.

I stand next to him by the sink and lean against the counter. We're so close that if he turned ninety degrees we'd be facing each other.

The water runs and I try not to be too aware of how he smells. Always just so faintly of cigarettes and warm laundry. For a guy who's a self-professed player, he almost never wears cologne.

The water splashes and Javi continues to ignore me until I look up and see his teeth are clenched so tight his jaw is popping. Damn, that's attractive. Among his many seductive qualities (the arms, the tattoos, the I-know-what-I-want-and-it's-you attitude), his jaw is near the top of the list.

I turn away from him, but not before he says something so low I almost don't catch it over the gurgling of the water from our crappy sink.

"I *don't* care."

Chapter Three

He doesn't seem to know what to do with himself after the dishes are done, the pots are scrubbed (better and more thoroughly than they had been in their entire pan lives) and the kitchen put back the way it had been, albeit cleaner.

"You can stay, if you want. I have to do homework, so it's going to be boring and I'm going to need complete silence," I say. Usually I go to the library with enormous noise-cancelling headphones, but since Shannon is gone tonight, I was going to take advantage and try to get ahead on some of my reading. The Socratic method of calling on random people for answers is something most of my professors utilize to terrorize their students into actually paying attention to the reading. And I'm sure as hell not going to look like a moron in front of an entire roomful of people.

He makes a sort of grunting noise guys do that can pretty much mean anything from "yes" to "fuck no."

"Suit yourself."

I go into the living room and start spreading my books out. Shannon doesn't understand why I don't read as much fiction as she does, but honestly, I have enough reading in my life already.

I don't look up when Javi appears in the doorway, stack of textbooks in hand. I don't look up when he settles himself on the floor, or when I toss him a pillow to use as he wishes.

He doesn't say a word, and I don't say anything either.

Usually once I have quiet, I can completely focus on my material. I always find things that everyone else thinks were boring, fascinating.

But that was before Javier was sitting on the floor in front of me, highlighter in hand, pen balanced on his ear and reading in a slouched (but still very sexy) position.

He isn't even *doing* anything. Just breathing and reading, his gorgeous eyes bouncing along the page. Ah, he's a fast reader. That explains a lot. I watch him out of the corner of my eye and either he's skimmed the page, or he's an even faster reader than I am. I'm going to bet the latter, and be green with envy.

"How's that homework coming?" he says, not looking up from his book as he highlights a passage. I can't see what subject it is, but the print is almost as small as my textbook and there aren't any pictures to break up the giant blocks of text.

"Fine," I say, my eyes going back to my page and trying to remember what was on it.

"It would go a lot better if you weren't studying me instead of the book." He makes another highlight and then looks up with a grin.

"Shut up. I wasn't studying you." I've been looking at him. That's totally different than "studying."

He rolls his eyes and goes back to reading and highlighting.

"Whatever you say, Haze." My heart always does a little flip when he uses my nickname. I can't help it, or I would definitely make it go away. I shouldn't get so excited by the sound of my own damn name.

Resisting the urge to chuck a pillow at him, or stick my tongue out at him, I glue my eyes back to my book and do my very best to ignore him.

Ignoring Javi is a full-time job in itself. It isn't anything he does, per se, it's just... him. His body taking up space and the sound of his breath and even minor movements that distract my peripheral vision.

I want to just give up, but I don't want him to know he's the reason I'm throwing in the towel. So I just keep trying to read and remember and not be distracted by him.

"Would it help if I went to another room?" he says, and I snap my eyes back on my book.

"Help with what?" I ask, not looking up.

"The fact that you've been undressing me with your eyes for the past ten minutes."

"I have not," I say, even though I definitely have been. But Javi is one of those guys you really want to undress. To see how far those tattoos go...

Javi chuckles and then slams his book shut, making me jump.

"I think I'm going to have some coffee, want some?" At this rate, if I have coffee I'll probably be up all night, but I'll probably be up all night anyway. My nocturnal work schedule messes with my sleep patterns and most nights it takes a long time for me to fall asleep.

"Sure," I say and close my own book.

Javi gets up and heads to the kitchen and after a second, I follow him. For a big guy, he moves really well. And hell, I've seen him dance. Javi in motion is a beautiful thing.

"Stop staring at my ass," he says, his back to me. It's like he has eyes in the back of his head.

"Stop being so full of yourself," I say, going to the fridge and looking for something to do. I stare inside and then grab a few apples and some string cheese.

Javi just shakes his head as he fills up the coffee pot and pours water in the machine.

"Want to have a smoke with me?" I shrug and we both head outside. This time he's the one with the lighter and he hooks me up.

"We really should quit," I say as we breathe out in unison, our smoke clouds joining and then dissolving into the night.

"We should," Javi says, but we keep smoking until we're down to the butts and stub them out in the bucket Shannon and I keep by the door.

"I will if you will," I say. I like the idea of doing something like this with Javi. A challenge that maybe I can beat him at.

"You mean that?" He holds the door open for me.

I shrug.

"Sure, why not? Make a contest out of it. They say you're more successful when you try to quit with another person." I'd read that in one of those pamphlets Shannon kept sneaking into my room when I wasn't home to subtly tell me I should quit.

"And what are the terms?" The coffeepot makes a horrible noise and then the fresh coffee starts pouring into the pot. I get out the mugs and hand one to Javi. Our hands brush and I try not to blush.

I'm not the kind of girl who blushes when she touches skin with a guy. Hell, I don't blush about much of anything.

But Javi makes me blush. I love it and I hate it.

"The loser…" I say, trying to think of something.

"Has to pose nude for the winner," Javi says and I make a sound of disgust.

"Classy."

"Hey, that would be more than enough incentive for me. How about you?" Sure, I'd love to see him naked. But I don't want him to know how much I want to see him naked.

"Loser buys the winner dinner? Or is that too cliché?" I say. Javi pours me some coffee and then pours himself some.

"Loser serves the winner dinner. Naked." He really wanted nudity to be part of this deal.

"No naked!" I yell and he just grins.

"Why not? It's so much fun." He's not even touching me, but I'm awfully turned on. Must be all the naked talk. I need to put the kibosh on that.

"For you, maybe."

"Oh, I think you'd enjoy it. Nudity usually leads to… certain activities that are more fun when you don't have any clothes on."

"Are you trying to seduce me, Javi?" I go for a joking tone, but the look he gives is pure sex.

"Yes," he says and sips his coffee. He's dead serious. No joking.

"Well, stop it," I say and have to turn away from him. I grab my snack and head back to the living room. Javi follows silently.

"Why?" he says when I sit down. He takes his place on the floor, but doesn't pick up his books.

"Because it's weird, okay?" I really don't want to talk about this. I never should have had him over.

"Weird how?" He won't let it rest, will he? I sigh and set my coffee down.

"Because… because it's wrong. I don't like it. So stop it." Only the first part of what I said is true. Javi and I would be an epic disaster. Sure, the sex might be good, but the aftermath? It would be awful and I'd definitely regret it. This is why one-night-stands with people you don't know very well are good. Like sexual Kleenex. Use once and throw away.

"You want me to stop?" he asks.

"Yes."

He shrugs.

"Okay."

"Okay?"

"Okay. I'll stop."

Chapter Four

Javi and I go back to our studying and I start to wonder how long he's going to stay as it gets later and later. Having another person around is less lonely, but I'm getting to the point where I want to take my bra off and put my pajamas on.

But I would dance around naked jamming to The Bangles before I would ask him when he is going to leave. However, I could heavily hint.

"It's getting late," I say, and fake a yawn.

"Uh huh," he says, not looking up from his book. He's been working away diligently, taking notes and highlighting and moving from one book to another. I should know, I've been watching him. Studying, but also watching him. I'm a good multi-tasker.

"Getting a lot done?" I say and he finally looks up at me. Shit. He's got a Study Face and… wow. Talk about attractive. I knew, even before he told me about his double major and minor, that Javi is smart, but seeing him in action is almost as much of a turn on as if he'd done a striptease.

Smart guys are hot. Period.

"Why do you want to know?" A smirk flits across his lips, but he suppresses it.

"No reason." I go back to my book and then yawn again. He chuckles and I look up.

"You're trying to kick me out. I get it, I get it." He stands up and starts gathering his stuff.

"I'm not kicking you out. It's just getting late. And don't you have better things to do?" And by "things" I mean "other ladies."

He shakes his head.

"Nope. I got nowhere to be. Jett and Shannon are probably on round two by now. She's loud, did you know that?" I cringe.

"Yeah, I've heard." She tries to be quiet, but then she's loud anyway. Sometimes I wonder if they're secretly filming a porno in there.

"But I'm happy for him. And her. They're definitely suited for one another."

"Definitely," I agree. Even though he's a mohawk-rocking, graphic t-shirt wearing, origami crane-making guy and she's an uptight, verbal-vomiting sweetheart. You'd never put them together, which, somehow, makes them perfect for one another.

"Well, I'll get out of your hair. Do you still want to do the quitting smoking thing? I'm up for it if you are. Loser buys the winner dinner. Twice."

Either way, that means I have dinner with Javi. There are worse ways to spend my time. Plus, it would allow me lots of ogling time.

"Sure. It's a bet. And I think we can trust each other to be honest? First one who smokes is the loser." I stick out my hand and he shifts his books to his other arm and shakes my hand. His hands are warm, like he's been holding them in front of a fire. Isn't there some saying about warm hands meaning a warm heart or something?

Javi squeezes my hand in his and then lets go.

"You can trust me, Haze," he says and I don't think he's just talking about the no-smoking bet.

"Goodnight, Javier," I say, and then feel like a total dork. I'm not some girl in a giant dress bidding adieu to her gentleman caller.

"Goodnight, Hazel," he says and then he does something totally unexpected. He leans forward and places the softest of soft kisses on my cheek. It's not even a peck, it's so gentle and brief. If I hadn't been on the receiving end of it, I might not have even noticed it. A total non-kiss.

But even that non-kiss sets my skin on fire and I have to fight the urge to grab hold of him, drag him to my bedroom and make him kiss me that way all over my body.

And then the bastard winks at me and whistles as he walks out the door.

"So, how was last night?" I ask Shannon the next morning when she stops by to change her clothes and take a shower before class. It seems silly that she comes all the way back to our place to do such things when she could have done both at Jett's.

"Ummm… let's just say we tried some new things." She giggles and blushes. Oh, sweet, innocent Shannon. She lost her virginity to Jett and he lost his to her. What's more is that they're in love, which, I'm told, makes sex better. I wouldn't know. I've never been in love with anyone I've had sex with. I've always been able to separate sex from love. Because you can have amazing sex with someone you're not in love with.

"Oh really? Details." I don't really want to know the details, but this is part of my duty as Shannon's BFF. Besides, I've shared plenty of my exploits with her, even when she begged me not to.

She doesn't tell me much, but I get the gist as I finish my second cup of coffee.

"I'm going to go shower," she says, glancing at the clock. She's going to have to rush if she's going to make it to her first class. I've scheduled all mine to start later in case I need to pick up an extra night at the bar during the week.

"Why don't you just do that at Jett's?"

She shrugs.

"I don't know. It feels weird. Like I'm living with him. And I'm not ready to be living with him." Yeah, sure. Spending every night together and most days is completely unlike living with someone.

"Yeah, I get that. So, I'll see you tonight?"

She shakes her head. "Can't. I've got to work and then I have a mandatory study group. Because showing up every day for class isn't enough anymore. I have to devote my outside of class time as well." She sighs and I give her a sympathetic look. I know all about that. Being pre-law requires so much out of class time it's a wonder I get any sleep.

"And Jett's coming back with me. Is that okay?" This is roughly the five-hundredth time she's asked me if it's okay that Jett comes over.

"No. It was cool all those other time's he's been over, but now I'm drawing the line," I say. Shannon narrows her eyes.

"Hey. I'm trying to be considerate. I've never done this boyfriend-staying-over thing and I want to make sure everyone is okay with it. Because if you weren't okay with it, that would be a problem. Because I want you to be okay with Jett. I need you to be okay with Jett." That's Shannon. Always wanting to make everyone happy. She's a much better person than I am.

"Sorry. It's good that you ask, but honestly, I'll let you know if there's a night I'm not okay with it. You are free to assume that I'm okay with it unless I tell you otherwise." She nods and heads off to the shower and I go back to the law book I'd propped up behind my bowl of cereal.

"Please tell me that's not one of those skim-sugar-latte things," a voice says behind me as I stir a packet of sugar into my coffee that afternoon. I don't need to turn around to know that Javi is standing behind me with one of those looks on his face. Like he's picturing me naked.

"It's black coffee with one packet of sugar. And what, you'd judge me on my coffee preference?" I say.

"Maybe." I roll my eyes.

"That's a really stupid reason to judge someone, Javier." He shrugs one shoulder. What is he even doing here? He doesn't have a coffee in his hand, so he must have spotted me and come over for no reason other than to harass me. As usual.

"How's the smoke-free life going?" I ask, hoping it will bug him, but all it does is make me want to go outside and have a smoke.

He inhales and then exhales deeply.

"Feeling good. How about you? No temptations?" Well, not before I'd seen him. I hadn't even thought about smoking until now.

"Nope. This is going to be much easier than I thought," I say with false confidence as I sit down at a table for two a girl with a huge stack of books has vacated. Javi sits down across from me without even asking if he can. That's another quality about Javier that makes me want to light a cigarette. He's way too confident for his own good.

"So, how's your day been? Cramming lots of information in that sexy brain of yours?" he says, watching as I drink my coffee.

"Well, it *was* going well."

He laughs.

"You love driving me crazy, don't you?" I say. Way to state the obvious, Hazel. Javi has enjoyed pushing my buttons since the day we met.

"If I said no, you'd know I was lying. It's fun riling you up." And now he's not just talking about making me irritated.

I sip my coffee and pretend I didn't hear him.

"Any exciting plans tonight?" he asks, completely ignoring the girl who walks by our table and gives him the once over. Interesting. I'm used to Javi openly ogling other girls. He's normally shameless about it.

"Just me hanging out with some sexy law books and taking notes," I say, wishing he would go away and let me enjoy my coffee in peace.

"Sounds like a party. I'll be by with dinner again. What would you like?" Wait, what?

"You don't have to make me dinner. I can make my own dinner." Well, I can order my own dinner and hand the takeout guy money, which is almost the same thing.

He waves off my protests.

"It's no big deal. I'm going to be making dinner for myself, so I might as well make a little extra and feed someone in need. You know, pay it forward." I almost toss my coffee in his face.

"You really know how to sweep a girl off her feet, you know that?" As always, my irritation only amuses him even more.

"I'll see you at six, Haze." He gets to his feet and saunters off. Because Javier can't just walk. He stalks, or saunters or marches.

And I'm left watching him and wishing I could have a smoke.

Chapter Five

Javi comes over and makes dinner for the rest of the week. Jett and Shannon join us on alternate nights and it's actually pretty fun having the three of them, even though it has sort of a double-date feel. Javi also enjoys making me squirm in front of an audience, so there's that to contend with. By the time Friday night rolls around, I would commit murder to go outside and smoke one cigarette. Just one.

"You okay over there, twitchy?" Javi says as Jett and Shannon clean up the plates. We're all going out later. The girls are coming over so we can all cram into two cars and I pulled the short straw so I have to be one the designated drivers. It's going to be interesting.

"What?" I say and realize my knee is jiggling up and down and I've been tapping my hand on the table. "I'm fine," I say with a huge smile. "I'm going to get ready."

"Need any help?" Javi calls after me and I slam my door in response.

As a result of working at a bar, I have a lot of clothes that work for going out. But tonight nothing looks right. Shannon knocks before she comes in.

"Whoa. What's happening in here?"

"Wardrobe crisis," I say, gesturing toward the clothes strewn everywhere.

"Wardrobe crisis? You? What happened to your usual attire? Cute top, leggings and BBs?" she says, referring to my usual outfit. My "bitch boots" are all lined up on the floor in my closet, just waiting to be stomped around in. But tonight I feel like… doing something different. I want to look sexy, but in a different way.

"I don't know. Could I maybe borrow something of yours?" Shannon's wardrobe is softer than mine. I tend to go for more bold colors and black than she does.

"Sure. If you can find something that will fit you." My waist is just a tiny bit slimmer than Shannon's and my torso is longer. But we both have plenty in the chestal region, so I might find something.

She leads me to her room and starts pawing through her drawers.

"What look are we going for?" she says.

"Sweet? Nice? Not a bitch?" Shannon gives me a look.

"Um, why? What's wrong with the way you usually look? You always look amazing." That is debatable, and beside the point.

"I don't know. I just want to try something different." I sit on her bed and pull off my t-shirt.

"Okay, sure. How about this one?" She holds up a light blue tunic that has a feather design across the front. "You could do it with your gray leggings and maybe some flats? And I have feather earrings if you want to go full-feather." I take the shirt from her and pull it over my head. It's so loose it does a *Flashdance* thing over one shoulder, which I like.

I stand up and look in the mirror. Not bad.

"Ugh, I hate how tall you are. It looks so much better on you," Shannon says with a sigh.

"Shut up, you know you're gorgeous. And I know a certain mohawked and tattooed Asian fellow out there feels the same way I do." She blushes at the mention of Jett. Adorable.

There is a bang as the front door opens and then I hear the voices of the rest of our group: Cass, Jordyn and Daisy, with one of Javi's friends, Marty, and Cass' boyfriend, Boyd. Jordyn has just broken up with her boyfriend (we all told her she'd dodged a bullet on that one) and Marty's trying to make a play for her, but she's sworn off men for the foreseeable future.

The gang is all here (minus Javi's buddy Skye, who is… somewhere else) and they are LOUD. But quiet friends are so boring. I skip back over to my room to finish my outfit and decide to wear my hair up instead of down. Might as well do the full makeover, and it's curling really nicely tonight. I go easy on the eye makeup, just doing a little bit of smoky shadow and lip gloss before adjusting my ponytail and leaving my room.

"Finally," Jordyn says. "You look gorgeous, girl!" I thank her and search the room for Javier. He's standing near the door, arms crossed and leaning against the wall. He's got a weird look on his face. I don't exactly know what it means, but I hope it's good. Jury is still out at this point.

"Okay, we're all here. let's go!" Cass yells and grabs Boyd's hand. We all pile into two cars, with me driving Jett, Shannon, Javi and Jordyn. Javi called shotgun, so he was next to me and of course Jett and Shannon wanted to sit together.

"Will y'all make sure Marty keeps his hands to himself?" Jordyn drawls from the backseat as she fluffs her already-fluffed hair.

"I'll have a little chat with him about respecting personal space," Javi says. "Don't even worry about it."

"I don't wanna be mean, but I just can't stand the idea of dating right now. I'd rather drink unsweetened tea." Shannon and I gasp in pretend shock.

"Oh, just shut up," Jordyn says and pouts. Our resident Southern Belle, you could take the girl out of the South, but you couldn't take the South out of the girl. She's always going to be asked where she's from the second after someone hears her thick southern drawl and her copious use of "y'all" instead of "you guys."

We spend the rest of the short drive to Hartford from our place in Deermont arguing about what to listen to on the radio. Since we're in Maine and one of the most popular activities to do is drink, we head for one of the only bars Shannon is comfortable going inside. As a bartender, I'm pretty much comfortable at the worst places. Honestly, the "bad" places aren't even that bad. Not really. But Shannon is weird that way and I want her to feel safe.

"I'm so glad I don't have to go trolling for losers," Shannon says with a sigh as Jett plays with her hair.

"No, you found one," he says and they do that cute couple thing where they stare at each other and I have to remind myself to focus on the road.

"Jealous?" Javi whispers so low no one can hear him over the radio.

"Nope," I say as I pull into the already-full parking lot and search for a decent spot.

I find one far away from the door and everyone cheers as I sneak the car into the spot and then turn off the engine.

The rest of the crew parks near us and we all merge again as we walk toward the door.

"You look really good tonight, Hazel," Javi says, his hand brushing my lower back as we go through the door.

"Thanks," I say as everyone else files in. And then, since I'm a bartender, everyone yells out their drink orders to me. I roll my eyes and take them and head to the bar. But I'm not alone.

"I don't need a helper," I say as Javi follows behind me, so close I keep bumping into him. "You know, I, like, make drinks for a living."

"It's crowded in here. I just wanted to make sure you got to the bar safely. Shit, yell at a guy for being chivalrous." That makes me laugh so loud a few people turned around and gave me dirty looks.

"You wouldn't know chivalry if it bit you on the ass, Javier," I say.

"You can bite me in the ass anytime you want, gorgeous," he says, leaning close and speaking in my ear.

Charming.

"How could I resist a line like that?" I say, turning around and finding his mouth close enough to kiss. Or bite, as the case may be.

"Why bother resisting?"

"I thought I told you to stop," I say, narrowing my eyes and taking a step backwards and bumping into the bar. I still haven't been able to order the drinks.

Javier sighs and backs off, holding his hands up in surrender.

"You got it." I turn back to the bar and try to get the bartender's attention. It takes a little while, and I'm half-tempted to hop over and mix the drinks myself. My friends have very simple tastes when it comes to alcohol. I'm always trying to get them to try different stuff, but they won't. Sigh.

Javier whistles so loud that everyone close to us turns, including the bartender, a guy who looks like he wouldn't know a gimlet from a martini glass full of dishwater. I give him the orders slowly, but I guess it isn't quite slow enough. At last, I have the tray full of drinks and lift it high over my head so I can carry it back to the table.

Javi doesn't ask to carry it for me, or else I might have shoved it in his face and then I'd have to deal with the stupid bartender again and wait for all new drinks.

Everyone claps when I arrive with the tray. We do the obligatory cheers and settle in to talk (yell) over the music. Javier's next to me, but he doesn't invade my space, which is nice.

After we all have a drink in us, the girls head out to the dance floor and then the guys follow a little reluctantly. Except for Javi. I know he secretly likes to dance. You can tell from the look on his face when he really gets going. He moves like he does everything else. With complete confidence.

The song changes to "Sex and Candy" by Marcy Playground. Talk about a throwback. The girls who have guys with them all pair up to do a slow grind. I look at Javier.

"Don't even think about it," I say, and move so I'm hip-bumping with Jordyn. And before I know it, a girl sidles her way up to him and then they're dancing in a way that might cause a pregnancy.

I go to glare at him and find him staring right at me. Not at the girl, who keeps pushing her ass into him. Wow. She's really going for the gold. But I can't exactly blame her. Javi is a great dancer and he's very easy on the eyes.

I feel my face go red and I try to stare right back at him so he knows whatever he's trying to do isn't going to work. If he's trying to make me jealous, I'm not going to be that easily swayed. One dance with another girl isn't going to change my mind. But he's welcome to try.

I grab Jordyn's arm and give her a little spin. We wobble a little bit from the drinks and then start laughing. Fortunately, the song ends and switches to something easier to dance fast to.

We dance our asses off until we're all parched and sweaty and need to sit down for a minute.

"Nice try, Javier," I say as I pass him to go get the next round of drinks. I'm done for the night, but I get a water to keep myself hydrated. This time he doesn't come with me.

We don't stay until last call, since a few of our group need to work the next day and want some time for recovery in the morning. I have to work tomorrow night, so I'm completely fine with this plan. My Saturday will consist of napping and homework. I'm really looking forward to it.

I drop Jordyn off first and then Javier. No one gets really wasted, thank God, so I don't have to worry about potential puke all over my upholstery.

"Good night," Javier says. Shannon gives him a little wave and Jett says he'll see him in the a.m.

"Bye, Haze. Thanks for the ride." He taps the roof of the car and gives me a wink before walking backwards to the rickety porch that leads to his and Jett's complete shithole of an apartment. I've been inside the place and the only way it could be improved is with a blowtorch. Burn that sucker down.

Shannon falls asleep on Jett's shoulder and he decides to carry her to bed. It's so sweet it almost shatters my heart.

"She's such a lightweight when it comes to booze," I whisper and Jett nods.

"Thanks for the ride. See you in the morning." I head to my room and strip off my clothes. I kind of want to take a shower, but I'll do it tomorrow.

The last thing I think about before I slip into sleep is the look on Javi's face while he was dancing with that girl.

I'm not jealous.

I'm not.

Chapter Six

'm not surprised when Javi shows up at the bar while I'm working. It's been an awful night. Too many drunk people spilling things and too many guys thinking they can just say what they want to me. My patience is gone by the time Javi leans on the bar and gives me a smile. And then he sees the look on my face.

"Whoa, rough night?"

"You have no idea," I say and then have to dash to the other end of the bar to pour another round of shots for a bachelor party. God, I hate bachelor parties. They almost never tip and they tend to get really drunk and sometimes handsy. I can handle drunk and handsy, but I'd rather not.

The next time I see Javi he's nursing a can of Bud Lite and pondering something so hard his forehead is all bunched up.

"What are you thinking about? It looks painful," I say, wiping the bar with a rag. There's a momentary lull and I decide to take advantage of it while I can and sip a glass of water.

"Nothing. Just… thinking." Wow, he's all serious. I'm not sure how to interact with a serious Javi.

"Anything I can help you with?" Why am I being nice to him? Ugh.

He looks up and shrugs one shoulder.

"Not exactly." I'm also not used to Javi being so non-talkative. He usually doesn't shut up.

"Need another drink?" If he won't talk to me, at least I can offer him liquid comfort.

He shakes his head and rests his forearms on the table. Even in the dim glow of the bar, his dark tattoos stand out against his skin, which is several shades darker than mine when I'm tan in the summer. I've never asked him what his tattoos mean. I don't have any tattoos myself. Never settled on a design I've wanted for more than five minutes so I figured it wasn't the best idea to put something like that permanently on my skin.

"Okay, dude, what's up? I haven't seen you look so morose in... well, ever." He smiles and I don't know if it's the fact that I called him "dude" or if it was my use of the word "morose."

"You don't have to bartender me. I'm a big boy. I can take care of myself. This isn't a movie." I roll my eyes and toss the rag in the sink.

"Fine. Reject my attempt to give you a proverbial shoulder to lean on. What are you doing here?" I cross my arms and ignore some guy at the end of the bar who has clearly already had too much and is signaling for more. I hate cutting people off, but it's one of the parts of being a bartender. I signal to Joe, my co-bartender. He's former military and has arms so big he can barely fit through a normal doorway. No one says no to Joe for fear that he'll squeeze their head between his hands until it pops.

"Just hanging out and drinking. Isn't that what people do in bars? Hang and drink?" Javi says. I watch out of the corner of my eye as Joe talks calmly and slowly to the drunk guy, who is drunk enough to argue with Joe, which shows just how impaired his judgment is.

"I guess. So you're not here to watch me and harass me?" My words sound harsh. It's really none of my business if Javi wants to sit here and drink.

"Am I harassing you? I'm not even doing anything." Now he's turned things around and I seem like the crazy one.

"No, just wondering about your sudden interest in drinking in the bar I work at on the nights that I'm working." He laughs.

"A little full of ourselves, aren't we? Maybe this has nothing to do with you." Bullshit. I call bullshit.

I just roll my eyes at him and head to mix another mojito for the girl on the end who is timidly trying to signal me.

Javi doesn't stay until last call, and I don't realize he's gone until his stool is taken up by someone else. He didn't even say goodbye. Maybe it isn't about me. But that still doesn't make any sense. That he'd come here when I'm here and sit at the bar. That isn't a coincidence.

After cleaning up and shutting down, I head home after saying goodnight to Joe and the rest of the crew. I fall into bed, and even though I'm exhausted, I can't seem to fall asleep.

I keep thinking about Javi and his mixed signals. Almost like he calculates every action for maximum annoyance and confusion.

I can no longer deny that there's something between us. Whether it's more than an attraction and a need for me to just have some dirty sex, I have no idea. This has never happened to me before, and I feel like I'm back in grade school and boys are a giant mystery wrapped in a riddle. I can't figure Javi out and it drives me to distraction.

Something is going to have to give sooner or later, and I have the feeling it's going to be explosive.

Javi is still quiet and thoughtful when comes over on Sunday to make dinner. Jett and Shannon are having dinner with us before going out on a date to the bowling alley. They ask if we want to come, but I'm too tired from work and I have a lot of reading to do. Javi mumbles something about a sore shoulder, which shocks me. Javi loves bowling because he's good at it and it's the perfect chance for him to show off in front of a large audience.

"What's up with him?" I say while Javi is in the bathroom. Jett shrugs and grabs a chip from the bowl I'd set out earlier as an "appetizer."

"He's just thinking about a lot. And the quitting smoking isn't helping. He's been kind of an asshole to live with, to be honest." Huh. So Javi is having a hard time quitting. Good. So am I.

On one of my breaks at the bar last night I'd actually gone out back to the smoking area and inhaled a few times, just to get the essence. It wasn't smoking if I just happened to be around someone else that was smoking. As long as the cigarette didn't touch my lips, I was good.

"Good. It hasn't been a picnic for me either." I really should stop talking about smoking. The more I talk about it, the more I want to do it.

"What's not a picnic?" Javi says as he comes back in the room and goes immediately to the stove to check the sauce he's making for the pork chops that are currently in the oven.

"Nothing," I say, not wanting to talk about the smoking thing anymore.

"You were talking about me, weren't you?" Javi says, pointing at me with the wooden spoon he'd used in the sauce and splattering it all over the floor. Shannon grabs a towel to clean it, but he takes it from her.

"I got it. My fault." He wipes up the spill and I hope he'll forget what he was just talking about.

"So, what were you saying about me?" he asks as he goes back to stirring the sauce. He isn't going to let it go.

"I was just asking how you were doing with the quitting smoking. That was it. Not everything is about you, Javier." Wow, I did not mean to sound like an uberbitch, but I definitely did right there.

Everyone stares at me.

"I'm clearly having trouble myself. One of the side effects of quitting smoking is irritability," I say. Plus, my period is due tomorrow. So it was really the worst idea ever for me to quit smoking this week. Way to go, Hazel.

"Sorry," I say, just for good measure.

He shrugs.

"Yeah, it's been rough. But talking about it isn't exactly helping, so how about we talk about something else. Anything else," Javi says and Shannon jumps in and starts talking about a girl who had a breakdown in one of her business classes and threw a fit so bad she had to be escorted out of the room by the teaching assistants. I send her a smile of thanks.

We eat and then the two lovebirds head out for bowling. I expect Javi to leave. But, of course, he just does whatever the hell he wants to.

"I have homework," I say, brushing crumbs off the table and onto the floor before I get up and start sweeping the kitchen, giving him the heavy hint that he might want to go.

"Me too. Brought everything with me." He dashes out to his car and then comes back with a stack of books and notebooks.

"You like to make yourself at home, don't you?" I say, dumping the dustpan in the trash and then putting the broom away.

"Your place is nicer than mine. And my place doesn't have you in it. So." He walks past me to the living room and starts spreading everything out on the floor.

I watch him, completely stunned. Am I reading too much into the "my place doesn't have you in it" comment? Probably.

"Okay then," I say, going to get my own books. "Let's study."

I do a lot better this time, but Javi is still distracting, even though he doesn't actually do anything to draw my attention away from my books.

Honestly, I don't have a ton of reading, so I finish quickly. Javi closes his last book and puts it on top of the stack to his left.

"Still have more to do?" he asks and stretches his arms, his shirt riding up to show some of his gorgeous stomach and a tiny bit of hair that I know leads downward.

"Nope, I'm done," I say, shutting my book. It isn't even nine o'clock. I'm definitely not going to bed yet. If Javi wasn't here, I'd probably put my pajamas on and watch a stupid movie. Ah, but he is here, so I can't do what I want. He's really been putting a crimp in my style.

We stare at each other for a minute and then he gets up.

"Want to watch a movie or something?" he says, going to the cabinet where we keep our DVDs and looking through them. He really has some boundary issues. Was he raised by wolves? I know nothing about Javi's home life. He's never offered any information and I'm usually too irritated by him to ask. Not that I've told him anything about my family either. I mostly try to forget about them. One of the reasons Shannon and I bonded early on was our somewhat crappy upbringings.

"I guess. If you want." I set my books on the coffee table, figuring he's going to want to sit next to me on the couch. "What did you have in mind?" He probably isn't going to find much that he wants to watch in our collection. Most of the movies belong to Shannon and she has a thing for John Hughes and romantic comedies.

"Yes!" he says, holding up a box. I can see what it is from the couch. *Step Brothers*. Nice. I figured it was either that or *The Hangover*. Or *Anchorman*. One of the trifecta.

"Nice choice. Put it in," I say and he gives me a look. "Oh shut up. You know what I meant." He just suppresses a laugh and puts the DVD in the player and turns the TV on.

"How many times have you watched this?" he asks as the movie starts.

"Um, probably more than you." I've seen this movie way too many times. In fact, I probably don't even need to watch it. I could act it out from beginning to end.

He settles on the couch, but far enough away that we're not touching. Wow, that's the first semi-considerate thing he's done since he got here.

The movie starts, but I'm not watching it. Without the distraction of homework, it's a lot easier to pay attention to Javi. He can't seem to get comfortable and keeps changing position.

"Will you sit still? Jesus." I glare at him and then grab a blanket from the back of the couch and throw it over myself.

"Sorry. So, you're not into blanket sharing?" He points to the blanket.

"You don't seem like a blanket guy." He laughs.

"What the hell is a blanket guy?" I roll my eyes.

"I don't know. Shut up and get under the blanket." I hold it up and he scoots over. This was not a good plan. Now he's much closer, since the blanket will only cover two people if they're sitting directly next to each other.

"You are shameless," I say as he rests his arms on the back of the couch and leans back.

"I have no idea what you're talking about," he says. "And shhh, I'm watching the movie." If I keep this going, he's only going to annoy me further, so I just cross my arms and slide as far away from him as possible, which pulls the blanket. He yanks it back to cover himself and then a blanket war ensues and the movie is forgotten.

"You're going to rip it," I say as I try to pull it back.

"Fine," he says and lets go so I fall back against the arm of the couch.

"You are such an asshole," I say, smacking his arm. He's just laughing at me.

"You enjoy it." I do NOT.

He's too close. And he's warm and he smells amazing and I can't stop thinking that I could just get up and climb on his lap and what else that would lead to.

I get up and throw the blanket at him.

"I'm making popcorn," I say, completely ignoring the fact that we ate dinner less than an hour ago.

"Extra butter and salt," Javi says as I head to the kitchen, his focus back on the movie as he wraps himself in the blanket like a burrito until only his face is showing.

"You're hilarious," I yell as I pull out the popper and get the popcorn from the cupboard.

"You know you enjoy it," he calls back. I would never admit it to him, but yes, I enjoy him teasing me. I enjoy having him here. And I sure as hell enjoy having him make dinner every night. I haven't eaten so well in… ever. I mean, Shannon is a decent cook, but Javi could be working in a fancy restaurant that had a snooty French guy at the door to turn people away who weren't fancy enough to eat there.

Since Shannon started dating Jett, she isn't around as much. That isn't her fault and I totally understand. But the apartment is lonely without another person in it. I never realized that I hate being alone. Even though I couldn't stand my family or my first insane roommate, at least there were other people around.

I measure out the popcorn and pour it in the popper and then go to the fridge for the butter and nearly crash into Javi.

"What the fuck?!" He must have shuffled from the living room to the kitchen while I'd been distracted.

"Just wanted to make sure you didn't need any help," he says, unwinding himself from the blanket. He's gone serious again and I open the fridge to put something between us.

"Well, next time, don't sneak up on me. It's rude," I say as I pretend to search for the butter, even though it's right in front of my face.

"Hogging blankets is rude too, Haze." Of course he has to call me Haze. I close my eyes and grab the butter and then slam the fridge shut.

"Inviting yourself over is rude, Javier." I hold the butter up like a sword. As if I'm going to impale him with it. What is wrong with me?

"Whoa, put down the butter, Haze. Think about what you're about to do. Think of your family," Javi says, holding his hands up in surrender. "Give me the butter and everything will be okay." I make a disgusted sound, but I go to hand him the butter. Instead of taking it, he grabs my wrist and pulls me close, holding the butter above my head.

"You're going to get through this." He's still doing the disarming butter bit, but I can't think of anything except how it feels to have one of his arms around me and to be up against his chest. I have no idea why he needed the blanket before because he definitely feels warm to me.

We stare at each other, both in suspended animation. Javi, holding the stick of butter up high and me, crushed against his chest. One of us is eventually going to have to move.

In the end, it's like we make a silent agreement. The butter drops to the floor and then Javi's mouth crushes against mine and I don't know if I kiss him, or he kisses me, but the point is that we're kissing and I'm on fire and I don't want it to stop, and I want it to stop because it's too much.

He's much too much. His mouth is too forceful, his arms grip me too hard and his tongue is too demanding.

But I'll be damned if I'm going to stop what is happening.

Chapter Seven

Javi makes a sound in his throat that's almost like a growl, and if it's possible, pulls me closer. And then things change. The kiss becomes sweeter, softer. He's got great lips, Javier. I like them much more when they're kissing me than when they're forming words designed to annoy me.

His hands move up my back and hold my face so delicately, it's like he's holding something he doesn't want to break. His tongue retreats, almost as if he's sorry for the initial assault and is waiting for me to decide if I want to continue.

It's the best and most confusing kiss I've ever experienced.

He starts to pull away and I make a sound of protest, and now I'm the one grabbing his face and attacking his mouth. He's only a few inches taller than me, so he doesn't have to bend in half to get to my lips.

He tastes like fire.

We bump into the fridge and then Javi starts walking us backwards. Well, backwards for him. The blanket falls away and somehow neither of us trips on it as we kiss our way to my door.

I've always seen that done in movies, but I never thought it was a thing real people could accomplish without crashing into something.

But here we are, at my door. Our hands both reach for the doorknob and it takes a few moments of groping to get it to twist the right way, and then we're falling onto my bed and then…

"Tell me this is real," he says, pulling his mouth away from mine, but only enough so he can speak. I open my eyes and am overwhelmed by his face dominating my vision.

"What?" I say, blinking a few times.

"Tell me this is real," he says again, brushing some hair off my forehead. "I've pictured this so many times that I want to make sure this isn't an elaborate hallucination. My imagination is good, but I don't think it's this good." He smiles a little.

"Well, unless this is some sort of dual hallucination, this is happening," I say. He has five freckles on his nose. I've never been close enough to notice before. I'm still trying to decide what color his eyes are.

"So this is happening," he says, as if he needs reassurance. What happened to the cocky Javier who danced with that girl the other night?

"Yes," I say, and to stop him from asking again, I kiss him. "It's real."

He's being so… sweet. I've never known Javier to be sweet before. I like it.

I keep thinking he's going to start pulling off my clothes, but he seems much too preoccupied with my lips. He sucks on my bottom lip and nibbles at it and then deepens the kiss, slowing it down even more. It's like he's trying out every kind of kiss and won't be satisfied until he's tested them all on my mouth. I'm more than okay with this. I've never been so completely and thoroughly kissed by anyone. If all we ever do is kiss, I can mark this in the win column. He shifts to get a better angle and I move with him, getting closer. I can barely breathe, but oxygen doesn't seem important. I taste the inside of his mouth and he tastes the inside of mine.

For the rest of my life, as long as I live, I will never forget this kiss. I curl myself around his body, wanting to be as close to him as possible. He sighs in happiness and smiles against my lips.

I inhale a deep breath. His lips are red and almost bruised. I put my hand to my mouth and find my lips in the same condition.

Neither of us knows what to say. And then he strokes my cheeks with his thumbs, kisses my forehead, both of my cheeks, my chin, under my jaw and both earlobes.

His tongue flicks out and tastes a spot just below my ear and I shiver. He can't know that's one of the spots that drives me crazy. But he does now. He chuckles and does it again and I sigh.

"Stop that," I say, but there is no force behind my words.

"No. You like it too much." He does it again and my fingers sink into his hair and I press myself closer to him. I want him so bad that any sort of reservation or reluctance has been destroyed by the need in my body. I have to have him.

Right now.

But Javier doesn't seem to feel the same urgency I do. He tries the same spot below my other ear and gets a similar reaction.

"Are you pleased with yourself?" I say, but it's mostly a whisper mixed with a moan.

"Very. I've thought about this for a long time." How long?

"Me too." Since the first time I saw him. That sounds romantic, but I only wanted to bang him at that point. Just once. Wham! Bam! Thank you, sir. And I'm pretty sure his first thoughts of kissing me had more nudity involved. But both of us still have our clothes on.

"This is weird," I say.

"That's a first," Javi says, leaning back. Crap, I didn't mean it the way he's taking it.

"No, no. That's not what I meant. The kissing was… I think mind-blowing would be an understatement. What I meant is that when

I pictured kissing you, I didn't picture it like this." He relaxes and props his head on his hand.

"How did you picture it?" Oh yes, he's pleased I've pictured us together.

"Well, I don't know." I hate being on the spot like this.

"Come on, Haze. You can't leave me hanging."

"Well, what did YOU picture?"

He smiles and his entire face lights up.

"This. Exactly this."

I give him a look.

"You pictured this? You, Mr. Take-Your-Pants-Off-Now pictured us fully-clothed, making out?"

He brushes his thumb across my lips and I have the urge to bite it.

"Haven't you learned by now not to listen to anything I say?"

"You confuse me," I say, but it comes out muffled against his hand.

"Hazel Gellar, you have no idea."

We kiss a little more but then we just sort of… hold each other. Javi runs his fingers through my hair.

"You have awesome hair, by the way," he says, wrapping a curl around his finger.

"Thanks, I grew it just for you." He laughs and then places a kiss on the tip of my nose.

"You're being really… nice. It's weird," I say.

"Thanks." I tilt my head up and look him in the eye.

"Don't be like that. I've just never seen you so… nice." That's really the only way to put it. He's gone from a guy I wanted to throw hot coffee on to a guy who is making me feel warm and comfortable and tingly all over. He's turning into one of those guys from Shannon's books. Saying the right thing, kissing me softly. Holding me close like he doesn't want to let me go.

"I didn't know you could be like this," I whisper.

"Well, I can." The question I wanted to ask, but didn't: Was he like this with anyone else? Or was it just me?

The next thing I know my alarm is blaring and I'm waking up on Javi's chest. He stayed the night. I don't even remember falling asleep, but here we are on my bed, his shirt clutched in my hands, his arms around my back. I've never spent the night with a guy. Ever. As soon as the sex was over, I left, or I made them leave. Sleeping (actual sleep, not sex) was far too intimate. When you sleep, you are at your most vulnerable. I would have sex with a guy before I'd let him see what I looked like first thing in the morning.

Javi sighs and shifts, his eyes opening slowly.

"Hi," I say, looking up at him. He looks down at me and it takes him a second to piece together the fact that he's in bed with me and it's now morning.

"Well. Good morning to you." He kisses my forehead and then closes his eyes as I turn off the alarm on my phone. "What time is it?"

"Seven. Sorry, I try to keep myself on a regular schedule so I get up early." He sighs.

"No worries. I don't have class until nine. But I should probably change my clothes." He looks down at his outfit from yesterday. Mine isn't much better.

"Yeah. And food. There should be food." I'm hungry and I have to pee, but I'm so comfortable I don't want to move. Plus, if I move then this thing might stop and I have no idea if we'll ever get this back again. Maybe Javi has a brain tumor and his sweetness is a side-effect.

"Take you out to breakfast?" he says.

"You don't have to do that."

He smiles.

"I know."

Since I'm the one lying on him, I have to get up first, so I do, groaning in the process. Javi gets up and stretches.

Luckily it's just the two of us since Shannon went to Jett's last night, so no one will be witness to this. But I'm sure Javi is going to tell Jett about it. Probably in great and lurid detail.

"How about this? I'll go back to my place and shower and then pick you up and we can go get something to eat." Javi says, gathering his books up from the living room.

"Sounds good," I say. "What are you going to tell Jett and Shannon?"

He shrugs.

"I'll say I was with a girl. Not a lie." He winks and starts to go for the door.

"Will you tell them it was me?" I call just as he's heading out the door.

"Do you want me to?" He pauses with the door halfway open, letting the cold air in.

"No."

"Okay, then." The door slams behind him and I head for the shower. The more time I spend with Javi, the more confused I become and the more I wish I could figure him out.

Chapter Eight

I have another wardrobe crisis for about three minutes and then mentally slap myself before putting on jeans and a sweater and pairing it with a scarf and a pair of BBs.

I'm ready and waiting for Javi when he knocks on the door.

"You knocked?" I say as I hold the door open. "You never knock. Is everything okay with you?" I'm only half-joking. There is definitely something different about Javi and I have yet to put my finger on it.

"Figured I'd be polite." Now? Now he decides to be polite? After all the other times he'd let himself in? Whatever. I don't have the brain space for this.

"Sure," I say and lock the door.

"I can be polite," Javi says as we walk down to his truck. It's "vintage" on a good day and a "POS" on a bad day. Still, it's better than that wreck Jett drives.

"Uh-huh." As if to prove his point, he shoves in front of me so he can open the truck door for me. Of course, this throws me off-balance and I nearly eat dirt.

"Wow, thanks. I nearly broke my nose, but at least I didn't have to open my own door." Javi laughs as I right myself and offers his hand to help me get in like he's a chauffeur or something. I don't take his

47

hand and get in the truck on my own, crossing my arms. The sweet, gentle Javier is gone and he's back to his old self. Last night must have been a fluke.

Javier gets in the driver's side and turns on the radio. I can't stop the disappointment from rolling through me.

"Lady's choice," he says, waving his arm at the dashboard as if bestowing a gift.

"How generous," I deadpan and flip through the stations until I find the oldies station I like that plays mostly eighties and nineties hits. They're currently playing "Vogue" by Madonna. I'll take it.

Javier makes a sound that says he doesn't exactly like my choice of music.

"You have a problem with Madonna?" I say as he pulls out of the parking lot and turns left. I have no idea where we're going for breakfast, but it's definitely not anywhere on campus.

"No, no. I have no problem with Madonna. None at all." Yeah, I totally believe him.

"Well, you said it was my choice and this is what I choose. So suck it up, Javier." He mutters something I don't quite catch.

"What was that?" I say.

"Nothing. Madonna is amazing," he grumbles and I just laugh. I'm much more comfortable with this Javier than whoever the guy was who cuddled with me last night. I don't know how to handle that guy. I can definitely handle this guy. Irritating Javier and having him irritate me back is familiar territory.

Javi takes me to a little coffee shop in Hartford that's not far from the bank where Shannon works.

"You going to order one of those sugar-skim-latte things?" I say as he opens the door of the truck for me.

"No. I'm going to order coffee that's blacker than my soul." He holds open the door of the establishment, which is simply called Hank's and not one of those kitschy coffee place names that always makes me want to gag. In addition to their extensive coffee menu, written on gigantic blackboards, they also have some of the most incredible-looking breakfast items, including little pies covered with whipped cream.

"I come here a lot," Javi says as we get in line to order. The place is packed, but there's not a laptop in sight. Weird. Super weird. I understand as we get closer and see a sign that says NO WI-FI. TALK TO SOMEONE.

"Yeah, they're not big on technology here. If you try to use a cell phone, they'll kick you out on the street. Even in the middle of the winter," Javi says in my ear.

Interesting. The coffee must be really good here to keep them in business. Nowadays it seems like you can't run a business if you don't offer Wi-Fi.

Javier goes first since I still need a minute to decide. He gets a black coffee and a chocolate chip scone and I have to stifle a laugh when he orders said scone. Because the last thing I ever thought Javier would eat would be a scone.

I order a black coffee as well and one of the little lemon pies. I'm an adult. I can have pie for breakfast if I want.

Javier and I get our coffees and plates of food and find a table near the window.

"So," I say, looking at the scone. "A scone, huh?"

"What? You're going to mock my breakfast choices?"

"Um, I do recall you mocking me for my potential coffee choices. So now we're even."

"Whatever," he says as he picks up the scone and bites into it. "Mmmm, scone." I grab my fork and start digging into my mini pie. It's pure heaven.

"Shit, this is good," I say with my mouth full. Javi just hands me a napkin and goes back to eating his scone with perfect manners. I take a few more bites of pie and then a sip of coffee before I ask the question that I've been putting off since we woke up this morning.

"What happened last night?" Javi sets the rest of his scone down and sips his coffee.

"What do you mean?" he asks.

"You know what I mean. The kissing and then the falling asleep. And now. What is this?" I wave my hands to indicate the breakfast buying.

He shrugs one shoulder and I want to strangle him.

"What do you think it is?"

"Don't answer a fucking question with a question," I say in a low voice so I don't disturb anyone with my cursing. "We both know something happened last night and I'd like to hear your side of the story."

He wipes his mouth with a napkin and then leans back in his chair.

"We kissed. We fell asleep. That's it." No, that wasn't it.

"You know that's not it, Javier. You don't kiss someone like that and then forget about it. You don't spend the night with someone like that and just forget about it." At least I don't. I've never done that with anyone. Not even in high school.

"So what are you saying?" He is absolutely trying to push every single button.

"I'm saying that... that last night meant something. Means something." Present tense.

"And what does it mean?" He leans forward and puts his arms on the table. He's got his sleeves pulled up to show his tats.

Why am I the only one having to answer questions? I asked him first.

"What does it mean to you?"

"I asked you first," he says. I'm about ready to flip this table. "I started this line of questioning and you have yet to give me an answer. So I'm not talking unless you start."

I cross my arms and lean back in my chair and press my lips together.

Javi smiles slowly, like he's amused by me. But I keep my mouth shut. I will not take his bait.

"Oh, that's how you're going to be?" he says. I say nothing. "I told you what happened. We talked, we kissed, we fell asleep. Don't try to make this something it wasn't." I'm not. I'm only trying to figure out what it was. Is.

"So you're saying that's all it was to you? Some making out and sleeping?" He nods slowly.

I don't believe him. The way we kissed last night and the way he looked at me... no. That wasn't just a kiss.

"You know my history, Hazel. You know I do things like kissing with a lot of girls." What is he doing right now? Last night he was so sweet and made me feel so special and now he's trying to act like I'm one of many. Either I am one of many, or he's freaking out. I really don't know which of the two it is, but my suspicion is the latter.

"Fine," I say. "Fine. You want to pretend like nothing happened, then we can pretend nothing happened." I go back to eating my pie. I can't look at him anymore.

I seriously want to cry and if I look at him, then I will.

Javi sighs and reaches out to me

"Don't. Don't you dare," I say, not looking at him.

"Shit," he says under his breath, but that's it. We both finish our breakfast in silence and ride back to my apartment in silence. He doesn't open the door for me this time. I feel rude not thanking him for the breakfast, so I do.

"You're welcome." And that's it. I get out of the truck and he drives away.

Shit.

Chapter Nine

Javi doesn't come over to cook dinner that night. Shannon stays with me, minus Jett. I ask why he's not coming over and she makes some sort of random excuse about him having homework, but I know better. She's seen the depressive state I've fallen into and decided I needed a friend tonight.

She's also cooking, which is probably a good idea since I'm so distracted my cooking would be even worse than usual.

We eat together standing in the kitchen, dipping our forks into the pot of chicken and broccoli pasta. Just like old times. BJ. Before Javier.

"So, what happened?" she finally asks as we scrape the bottom of the pot.

"Nothing," I say. I don't want to talk about it. I just want to forget it even happened. Wipe it from my memory. Hit the Delete button.

She pokes my arm with her fork.

"Ouch. Eat the pasta, not me."

"What happened? Because you were happy yesterday and you're not happy today and Javier was acting all weird this morning and I have the feeling that you guys did something last night. I'm not judging, but I want to know so I can help you make it better." How someone like me scored a best friend like Shannon, I'll never know.

"Nothing happened. I mean, not really. We kissed a little and then fell asleep and then we got up and he took me out for breakfast. That was it." I shrug one shoulder, trying to brush it off.

"And? That was it? Are you like, together now?" I could definitely answer in the negative on that.

"No. I asked him if it meant anything, and he said no. So it was nothing. Honestly, I want to forget about it and just go back to the way things were. Javi annoys me, I annoy him. It worked. I just want to go back to that. God, I hope we can go back to that." We might be able to hit reverse since we only kissed.

"Wow. So you didn't have sex?"

"No, Shan, we didn't. We just kissed a little." A lot.

"Huh. Well, how about that?" She stabs the last piece of chicken and grins at me.

"I'm capable of not having sex with someone, you know," I say.

"I know. I'm just surprised. I mean, you were the one who said you wanted to use him to clean out your pipes." I roll my eyes. I should have kept my mouth shut about wanting to bang Javi.

"I know, I know. But he's… I don't know. He's…"

"Javier," she supplies. Yup. That's the only explanation. He is who he is.

"So, was it good?" she asks. "The kissing, I mean. I'll stop asking about it, promise." She definitely won't stop asking. Shannon has a bad habit of mentioning things that probably shouldn't be mentioned. It's like she doesn't have control of the words that come out of her mouth. But I love her anyway.

"This kissing was… it made all the other kisses I've ever had seem like practice." It was thorough, perfect and the the memory of it made my skin tingle.

"Your lips are a little red," Shannon says while I wash out the pot and our forks.

"Are they?"

"Uh-huh." I put my hand to my mouth. My lips are still tender and oversensitive. Wonder how long that's going to last.

Shannon and I do homework together and then watch a movie.

"Anything but *Stepbrothers*," I say. I'll never feel the same about that movie again. Fucking Javier. Now he's ruining movies for me.

"Okay, I'm not going to ask. How about something new?" She's clearly been waiting for this moment and rushes to pull out a DVD box I don't remember ever seeing before.

"I got this last week at the thrift store and I've been dying to show it to you so we could watch it together." It's a box set of the first season of *FRIENDS*. "I found it hidden on a shelf. You in?"

"Hell yes, I'm in," I say. "You don't even need to ask." She makes a little sound of glee and puts in the first DVD.

I settle into the world of Monica, Chandler, Phoebe, Joey, Rachel and Ross and for a little while, someone else's relationship problems occupy my mind. But Javi is never far from my thoughts.

I can't stop flashing back to our kiss and the aftermath. When I go to bed tonight, my sheets are going to smell like Javi. I can't decide if I like that or not.

Shit, I need to smoke.

"You're twitching," Shannon points out. I can't help it.

"Sorry. I'm stressed and I can't smoke, so I'm twitchy. It will get better, I promise." I have no idea if it will get better, but I'm not losing this stupid bet to Javier. Hell to the no.

"Maybe you should take up knitting," Shannon says. I give her a look. "You know, keep your hands busy. What is it they say about idle hands? They belong to the devil or something. I have no idea." Neither of us was raised with a working knowledge of the Bible.

"I have no idea either, but they say it's supposed to get better," I say, cracking my knuckles.

"Maybe you should try the gum? Or the patch?" I shake my head.

"No, that stuff is more for people who smoke a lot, I think. I shouldn't be having this hard of a time with it. I have no idea what's wrong with me." Shannon gives me one of those "knowing" looks.

"What?" I say.

"I think it has less to do with quitting smoking and more to do with other things." I know exactly what she means by "other things." She means "other thing" and by "other thing," Javier.

"It's not other things. It's just that I need nicotine in my life and I don't have it right now. That's it." I cross my arms to stop my hands from twitching, but then my feet start going. I can't win.

"Maybe some tea or something? Settle your nerves?" I'm clearly bugging Shannon, so she gets up to make some tea for me. Tea definitely isn't going to help with this situation. Not much will.

Shannon comes back with two cups of tea that's supposed to help you sleep, but will probably just make me want to pee. I drink it anyway.

We get halfway through the set of DVDs when Shannon falls asleep on the couch. I might be able to carry her to bed, but I tap her shoulder instead.

"Sorry, babe. I wasn't sure if I could get you to bed." She nods and I walk her to bed and then go back to turn off the TV. I'm not the least bit tired, mostly due to the great night's sleep I had last night.

I turn on my back and close my eyes, trying to think of something soothing, like ocean waves or crap like that. It doesn't work, so I turn on my side and then try the other side and then my stomach.

Nothing works.

At this rate, I'm going to be up the whole night. I take a deep breath and all I can smell is Javier on my pillow.

My phone buzzes with a text message.

Can't sleep. Come over?

It's from Javier. This is the first time he's ever texted me. I read it through a few times to make sure I have it right.

He wants to come over? I get up and look out the kitchen window. Sure enough, his car is sitting in the driveway.

I chew on my lip and wince.

I'm not okay with the crap he put me through this morning. But last night...

If you promise not to be an asshole.

He gets out of the car and walks to the door, feeling under the flowerpot for the spare key. But I open the door and put my finger to my lips.

"Shannon's asleep," I whisper. He just nods and follows me inside and to my room. I shut the door and he shucks off his coat and shoes.

"Why are you here?" I say in a low voice. I don't want Shannon to know he's here.

"I couldn't sleep," he says and pulls off his pants, leaving him wearing only a t-shirt and boxers.

And then he climbs in my bed and holds the covers up for me.

"You can't just get in my bed, Javier."

"I just did. Get in. It's cold." It's not cold, but I get in anyway, turning on my side to face him. His eyes are closed and he puts his arm around me, pulling me close.

"Please don't be mad at me," he says into my hair. "I just don't want you to be mad at me."

I'm always mad at him. He drives me crazier than anyone ever has. But lying here with him, my head is quiet and my body is calm and warm. It feels the same as last night.

"Just don't be an asshole and I won't have to be mad at you," I say, moving closer to him and putting my hands on his chest.

"I'll do my best," he says and then sighs. My eyes close and I listen to the beat of Javi's heart. Much better than ocean waves.

When I wake in the morning, Javier is gone. I grope around my bed for him, but he's nowhere to be found. I open my eyes and look around. My hand closes on a note he's left on the pillow next to my head.

Thanks for last night. I'll do my best to make it up to you. See you tonight for dinner.

-Javi

I sigh and push my hands through my hair. I don't like waking up and not having him here. I know how crazy that sounds. He's slept in my bed all of two nights and I can't figure out how I slept before. You'd think it would be the opposite, that having someone in my bed would make sleeping more difficult. But no, I have to be a weirdo.

I can't tell Javi how much I want him to stay the night with me. It would sound way too desperate and needy. Still, he was the one who texted me and asked to come over. And I was the one who let him in.

Javi and I are definitely going to have to sit down and have a serious talk about what the hell we are to each other now. Things have changed and everything is all… weird.

Crap. I probably shouldn't have let him kiss me. Or kissed him. However that happened. I don't really remember. And I definitely shouldn't let him sleep in my bed again.

Well, fuck.

I stumble out to the kitchen to find Shannon at the waffle iron and Jett sitting at the table, his hair already gelled to perfection.

"Don't go near any open flames," I say to him as I sit in my chair. "Your head is definitely flammable."

He just grins at me and sips his coffee.

"I'll take the risk."

"I like your hair," Shannon says, pouting a bit. "I mean, any way you wear it, but I love it when you spike it up. It's... you." She leans down and gives him a kiss.

"Thank you, princess." I try not to gag at the pet name.

"Waffles?" Shannon asks. I nod and then pour myself some coffee. It's a really good thing I have so many people around me who can cook. Otherwise, I'd probably starve. How I've been able to manage this long is still a mystery.

I dig into my waffles in silence, but I can feel Jett and Shannon staring at me.

"Stop it. You're both being creepy." I look up and find that yes, they are both giving me weird looks.

Shannon blushes and Jett looks at his waffles.

"I know Javi was here last night," he finally says. "I heard him drive out in the middle of the night and figured out where he was going." Shannon and Jett share a look and it tells me that they've been talking about Javi and me behind our backs. Nice.

"I shouldn't have to explain any of this to you, you know. It's not really any of your business." When Shannon was "fake-dating" Jett, I used to want to know everything. Well, now the shoe is on the other foot and I know how awful it feels.

"You're right. I just want to make sure you're okay," Shannon says. "We care about you and Javi." I know they do. But right now their care is making me want to go outside and smoke so I can escape the scrutiny. I don't like this at all.

"I don't want to talk about it. When/if I do, I'll let you know," I say and stab my waffles.

And that is the end of that. Jett and Shannon talk about other things, and Shannon asks if I mind if Jett has dinner with us tonight. I say that I don't and then Jett folds his napkin into a crane and puts it on my plate.

"Thanks. Sorry for being crabby. I just… I don't know. This is all confusing." The crane starts soaking up the syrup left on my plate and droops.

"Been there, done that, read the book, saw the movie adaptation and the awful sequel," Shannon says. "I'm here if you want to talk. And I'm sure Jett wouldn't mind helping you decipher the mystery that is Javier."

"I absolutely volunteer," Jett says, raising his hand. "I have quite a bit of Javier experience and I'm happy to share."

They're both sweet, but I think this is one of those things I need to figure out on my own.

"I appreciate it, but I think I'm good. I'm going to take a shower," I say and Jett takes my plate to the sink.

Chapter Ten

Javier arrives as planned, with a bag of groceries.

"Where the hell are you getting the money for all this food?" I ask. He shrugs one shoulder. I hate it when he does that. It's such a non-answer.

"I have my ways," he says, dumping the bags on the kitchen table.

"So you're secretly a billionaire? You wouldn't know it from that place you live in." That apartment makes me shudder. I have no idea how Shannon can spend so much time there. I'd have to wear a Hazmat suit just to spend the night.

"Shhh," Javi says, putting his finger to his lips.

"Seriously, though. Where are you getting the money for all this?" Javi is always vague about money. As far as I know, he doesn't have a job.

"Don't worry about it."

"I'm not worried, I just want to know, Javi. I mean, it seems a little crazy for you to be buying all our groceries." Shannon and Jett emerge from her room, hair and clothes in disarray and sheepish looks on their faces. Javi whistles at them and they both go redder.

"Might wanna fix your hair, man," he said, motioning to Jett's messed up hair.

"Be right back," Jett says and Shannon pretends to stare at something on her hands.

I just help Javi unload the groceries and start dinner. I wouldn't say I'm ready to be on *Iron Chef*, but I'm getting much better at not ruining whatever I'm cooking. And I now know the difference between cast iron and regular pans. Mostly thanks to Javier's lectures. Passionate about pans, that guy.

Shannon and Jett get over their embarrassment and are back to their normal selves in a few minutes.

"So we were thinking that we should have a party or something some weekend instead of our usual bar-visiting," Shannon says. "You know, something pre-finals, just for fun. Have everyone over, cook some food, have a few drinks, etc. What do you think?" She's asking me.

"Sounds good. I'm guessing you want to have it here, yes?"

"Well… Jett and Javi's place isn't really fit for a party of more than a few people. And I just think it would be nice, you know?" Shannon seems so happy, and she wants to share it with everyone. Nothing wrong with that, I guess.

"Sure, we can have it here."

"Maybe I can barbecue," Javi says. "I've got a little portable grill that I haven't been able to use because there's no flat surface outside for us to use it, so it's been sitting in my closet forever." Javi's eyes light up at the prospect of barbecuing.

"Yeah, sure. We should be able to fit something on the porch." He won't have a lot of room to move around, but it will still be better than using it at his place. I wouldn't put anything of value on that porch.

"Awesome!" Shannon says.

"Just not on Saturday since I'll probably have to work." If we do it on Sunday, I'll probably be hung over on Monday, but I'd rather that than be hung over at work.

"Works for me," Shannon says and she and Javi start planning the menu. I can't tell who is more excited. It's a toss-up.

I just go back to watching the boiling potatoes. Javi gets the steaks going and Shannon and Jett make a chopped salad.

I want to talk to Javi and ask him if he's coming over to spend the night tonight, but I'd rather not have an audience, so my question will have to wait.

Dinner is uneventful and then it's time for everyone to do homework. Jett and Shannon decide to stay, so the living room is crowded with books and notebooks and laptops.

Jett's working on a project for one of his graphic design classes and keeps asking for opinions and Shannon's trying to design a marketing campaign, so I keep getting interrupted. I don't mind, though. It's nice having the apartment full of people. Besides, I'm not behind, so it doesn't matter how much I get done tonight anyway.

Javi is quiet again. Not surly or mad. Just quiet.

Once again, I'm not used to dealing with a quiet Javi. So I ignore him for the most part, since that's what he seems to want.

We all work for hours, and by the time Shannon and Jett are ready for bed, Javi hasn't said anything about staying or going.

"See you in the morning," Shannon says, blowing me a kiss. Jett gives us both a salute before they head to Shannon's room and shut the door. I wait a few minutes before I speak.

"Are you going to stay?"

Javi closes his book and gets up, gathering his books and then he leaves the room. The front door slams and I'm left sitting on the couch and wondering what the hell is wrong with him. I didn't even say anything. God, what a jerk.

Well, fine. If he wants to be an asshole, he can be an asshole. At his place.

I'm startled as the door slams again and Javi comes back in with a backpack.

"Ready for bed?" he says.

"What the fuck, Javi?"

"I had to get some stuff from my car," he says, as if I've asked something ridiculous.

"You're staying?" He just nods and heads to my room. "I didn't invite you to stay," I say, following him and closing the door as he starts to pull things out of the bag. Toothbrush, clothes, etc. Like he's having a sleepover.

"I thought you wanted me to. But I can go." He starts putting the stuff back in his bag.

"No, no. I just... you aren't very good at communication sometimes, Javi. And for someone who never shuts up, that's a little weird. I'm confused here, and you're not making that confusion get any clearer." In fact, I have a headache coming on.

"I mean, making dinner is one thing, but just inviting yourself over to sleep in my bed is weird. Not saying I don't want you here, I just want you to consult me before you make decisions that involve me. I don't think that's too much to ask, honestly." He watches me as I talk, his face blank. But I see the words getting through to him. He sighs and his shoulders slump a little.

"You're right, Haze. I'm sorry. I've just had a shitty day and... I don't know. This whole situation is something I've never dealt with before and I don't know how to handle it."

"Yeah, well, that makes two of us. But you can't shut me out and also expect me to go along with whatever. Relationships don't work that way." He sits down on my bed and I sit next to him.

"So this is a relationship now?" he says, bumping my shoulder and smiling.

"You know it is. I have no idea what kind of relationship it is, but it's... something." No idea what to call it. Friends with benefits? But we aren't having sex, so the only "benefit" right now is the sleeping.

"Yes, it's something." He brushes my hair over my shoulder. "I'm not very good at… sharing what's going on inside my head."

I roll my eyes.

"Unless it's sexual, right?"

He laughs.

"Right."

"Shh, I don't want Jett and Shannon to overhear," I say in a low voice. I could almost picture them with their ears up against the wall.

"I'm pretty sure Jett and Shannon are currently only concerned with Jett and Shannon," Javi says in my ear before kissing my earlobe.

"Stop that," I say, trying to push him away. "You can't just kiss my ear, Javi."

"Why not? You like it, I like it. Win-win."

I turn to face him.

"Because you're not my boyfriend. I'm not your girlfriend. I'm not even sure we're friends. This whole thing is completely confusing and before it goes forward, I want to know what you want from me."

He sighs again.

"I don't know what I want. I just… I like being with you and staying the night with you and I sure as hell liked kissing you. But I keep thinking if we take this to the next level, I'm going to fuck it up and then it's going to make everything awkward. I mean, Shannon is your best friend and Jett is mine and that could make things really suck for them." He has a good point, but it's almost as if we've passed the point of no return. Things have already happened, and if we pretend like they haven't, we're both liars.

"What makes you so sure you're going to fuck it up? Maybe I'll be the one to ruin things." This is just as probable.

"No, I think it would be me, Haze. I'm kind of volatile when it comes to women. There's a reason I'm one and done when it comes to sex."

"Well, join the club. I'm not exactly a fantastic girlfriend either. Hell, I can't even remember the last time I actually had a boyfriend."

"Well, I'd make a terrible boyfriend." He leans closer to me and heat sparks between us.

"Okay, so you make a bad boyfriend and I make a bad girlfriend. So how about we ditch that whole thing and just... do whatever? There's no law that says we have to define anything, or behave a certain way. We can just... be together when we're together and be not together when we're not together. I don't need a boyfriend. Shit, I don't have time for a boyfriend." That is an understatement. I need someone to have sex with me and make me dinner and take me out every now and then. Some people might call that a boyfriend, but I'm not asking for exclusivity.

"You'd be fine with being... together-ish?" I laugh. That's the best way to put it.

"Sure. As long as you're safe. And I'll be likewise." Sure, I'll have casual sex, but I'm not playing with my health. That's just stupid. I've never had sex without a condom. Doing so prevented me from having sex a few times, but I'm not taking any risks.

"Always. I never leave the house without protection." He's dead serious. No joking. He reaches into his back pocket and pulls out a condom.

"Is that supposed to impress me?"

"No. Just to show you that I'm always prepared." He puts it away.

"Were you a boy scout?"

He chuckles.

"Believe it or not, I was kicked out of the boy scouts. That's another story for another time, though. I'm tired."

"Yeah, me too," I say, but it's a lie. I'm not tired. I'm turned on and I really want to have sex right now. Lose myself in the sensations in my body for a little while. Javi is here and I think if I push him in the right direction, he'll be all for it.

"Sooo," he says, pulling out his clothes to sleep in.

"Sooo," I echo, standing up and pulling my shirt over my head. Might as well make my intentions clear. "I sleep naked most nights. Want to give me a hand?"

Chapter Eleven

I turn slowly and look over my shoulder at Javi. All he has to do is reach out and unhook my bra and slip my panties over my hips.

"Javi?" He's staring at my back like he's never seen one before.

"Javier."

His eyes snap up to mine. This seduction thing is a lot more work than I thought it would be.

"Are you sure?" he finally asks. "Don't get me wrong, this is something I've fantasized about a lot. Too many times to count, but…" He looks so vulnerable in this moment that I almost want to give him a hug.

I turn around and tilt his face up.

"I have faith in you, Javier. But if you don't want to, then we won't." He's staring at my lips.

"I've never turned down sex before," he says. "Feels wrong."

"It's okay," I say. It looks like tonight won't be the night. I should probably put my clothes on.

I reach for my shirt, but Javi grabs my arm. Our eyes meet again and I can almost see the wheels clicking in his brain.

"Fuck it," he says and yanks me down on top of him, smashing his mouth to mine so hard I nearly bite through my lip.

Well. That's a change in direction, but I'm totally with him. My bra is practically ripped off me and my panties join the rest of my clothes on the floor.

"Not fair," I say against Javi's mouth. There's nothing safe or sweet about these kisses. They're all about claiming and taking and wanting.

I run my hands across his chest and start pulling his shirt over his head. We have to break the kiss for a moment and then we're back at it.

I'd love to look at him as he undresses and all that, but this isn't the time.

I break two fingernails undoing his belt, and then his pants are on the floor and he's naked and I'm naked and good GOD it's been a long time since I had a sweaty man above me.

His tattoos are absolutely amazing. They extend from the center of his chest, over his shoulders and down his arms, almost like tribal wings. He's even more gorgeous than I thought he would be.

I pull my mouth away from his so I can kiss his neck and then his chest. Sounds of pleasure rumble through his chest and I flick my tongue out and taste one of his nipples.

"Shit, Hazel." I do it again and he closes his eyes. Ha. I like having the upper hand sometimes.

But then Javi decides he wants to swap and pulls my mouth away and starts kissing down my neck, stopping for a moment to suck on that spot below my ear that drives me crazy. I moan and hold onto him. Hell, he could make me come just from doing that.

His searing lips move lower and then he takes one of my nipples into his mouth and I dig my fingers into his scalp. He chuckles and the sound vibrates against my sensitive skin. He's undoing me. The combination of not being with someone for ages and the anticipation I've built up for this moment have ignited me and I can barely stand it.

While his mouth is working on my upper half, his hands are drifting lower and my entire body is shaking, waiting for him to touch me. When he does and I arch into him and it's so damn good. Touching yourself is one thing, but having someone else do it (someone with nice big hands and excellent fingers) is on a whole other planet.

One finger goes inside me and then another as his thumb works at my clit. I know he's done this before and I'm glad. I don't have to draw him a map, or pretend to be gyrating in pleasure as he fumbles around. Javi knows exactly what he's doing and just like when he irritates me, he's pushing all the right buttons.

I come so fast that I cry out in surprise. God, that has to be a record. Javi pumps his hand, prolonging the sensation that rockets through my body and leaves heat and tingles and glowing beauty in its wake.

He's wrecked me. Ripped me apart. I pant and he gives me a second to recover.

"Thank you," I say.

"You're welcome," he says with a chuckle as he licks his fingers. "Mind if I taste you?"

"By all means," I say and then he puts his mouth on me. I almost push him away because I'm so sensitive to the touch of his lips and tongue it almost hurts. But the momentary pain gives way to the building of another climax. Relentless he adds his fingers again, driving me hard and fast toward another orgasm.

I thrust my hips toward his face, and I hope he can breathe, but I don't really care about that at the moment. All I care about is throwing myself off the edge of the cliff again. I just want to fly.

Javi buzzes his lips against my clit and thrusts hard with his hand and that's it. I'm spreading my wings and soaring.

My chest heaves as Javi makes his way back up my body, leaving little kisses here and there.

"Thank. You."

Javi laughs and kisses the tip of my nose.

"You said that already. And you don't have to thank me every time I make you come. I enjoy it almost as much as you do." He's slowed down again and doesn't seem to be in a hurry to jam himself inside me, unlike some guys I've been with.

"Well, it's not often a guy can get me off twice in that short amount of time. You've clearly been practicing." He runs a finger between my breasts and circles my navel, making my skin break out in goosebumps.

"All that practice, just for you," he says.

"Well, yay for you. And now it's time for me to show you what I've learned in my own studies." I shimmy down until my face is level with his dick. I've never been very fond of the blow job, but for Javier, I'll make an exception. Honestly, the idea of getting him off makes me excited.

"You don't have to," Javi says. I just look up at him and stick my tongue out, licking him just at the tip. His eyes close and his head rolls back. A moan comes from his mouth and I do it again, eliciting the same reaction.

I decide to give him the full treatment instead of going right for the kill. I want to take my time, to show him I appreciate what he did for me.

So I do. I start out slow with my tongue, tasting him everywhere before I add my hand, moving up and down in time with my licks.

He makes a strangled sound when I finally take him into my mouth as far as I can go without gagging. Then he lets loose with a string of curses that almost makes me laugh.

I work slowly up and down, but he stops me before I've even got a good rhythm.

"I want to be inside you," he says, pulling me up to kiss his mouth. Works for me. But someday, I will give Javier a blow job and it will probably be someday soon.

He gets his pants and pulls out the condom from his back pocket. Even if he didn't have one, I have a few extra in my dresser drawer. I never like to be unprepared when it comes to sex.

"I'm okay with that," I say as he rolls the condom on and then positions himself over me.

"I just want to warn you that I sometimes get a little... intense. Just yell at me or slap me or something if it gets to be too much."

"Um, sure. I'll let you know."

He smiles.

"Good." He brings his mouth back to mine and then pushes into me. He feels so good I wrap my legs around him and squeeze my hands on his ass to bring him closer. Javi fills me and every muscle in his body strains to keep himself still.

"You're not going to hurt me, promise," I say. I like rough sometimes and this is one of those times. "Please, Javi."

He nips at my lower lip.

"You asked for it." And then he slams his hips into mine, rocking me back into my pillows. Okay, he wasn't joking. Before I can even take a breath, he's pulling nearly all the way out and thrusting into me again. Oh, GOD.

"Faster," I say, and he obliges, picking up the pace and then thrusting so hard my head bangs against the headboard. I move my pillow up so I don't break my neck, but I don't ask him to slow down. I've never been fucked this hard, and it's not hard enough.

Javier fucks me like he's trying to tear me apart. I. Love. It.

By now both of us are being quite loud and Javi is going so hard that my bed is banging against my wall. Then there's a crack and suddenly we both fall a few feet.

I gasp and Javi curses.

"You broke my bed," I say and Javi looks down at me. His eyes are dark and clouded. Takes him a moment to realize what's just happened.

"I'll buy you a new one," he says and then resumes his activities. I could tell him to stop, but I can't find a reason. The damage is already done so we might as well finish what we started.

One screaming climax (for both of us) later and there is a knock at the door.

"Is everything okay in there?" asks Shannon's timid voice. "We heard, um, a crash. We just wanted to make sure you're not maimed or injured in any way."

Javi is still inside me.

"Are you maimed in any way?" I ask, trying to keep a straight face.

"Nope. Everything is great. Right where it should be." He grinds his hips a little and I wonder if he's getting hard again. "Are you maimed or injured?"

"Well, there's something that wasn't there before, but I don't quite want to remove it yet. Other than that, I'm good." Javi swirls his hips and yup. He's getting hard again. I'm up for round two, but I don't think my bed is.

"We're both fine," I yell.

"Okay. Good." Shannon says and I can hear her talking in a low voice to Jett. Oh, this is so much fun.

"We're fine," Javi says, shaking his head at them.

"Okay. Well. We're going back to bed," Shannon says.

"Have a good night," Jett adds. Javi and I listen as they go back to Shannon's room and close the door.

Javi looks down at me and I start laughing.

"Whoa, keep doing that and there's going to be more bed breaking." That's probably not the best idea then.

"Well, I'm kind of between a rock and a hard place." More like a bed and a hard place.

"You love my hard place," he says, but then he pulls out.

"We should probably do something about this," Javi says, indicating the bed. My bed is split in half, the wooden frame completely buckled. Well, I did get it at a garage sale, so that's what I get for buying cheap furniture.

First though, we might want to put some clothes on.

He rolls off me and grabs a tissue to take care of the condom before putting his pants on, sans boxers. I grab his shirt and throw it on and we begin shifting the broken bits of bedframe against one wall and then settle the mattress on the floor. I have to move a bunch of the stuff I've stored under the bed, and I try to hide some of it from Javi. It's not fair that he gets to see all the intimate details of my room. But this isn't a typical relationship, so I guess those rules don't apply anyway.

"Guess we should go to bed," Javi says as we pull the blankets up on the makeshift bed.

"We should. Or," I say, going to my dresser and pulling out an entire strip of condoms, "we could try to break through the floor and make it into the apartment downstairs." I throw the strip at Javi and he catches it.

"Well, we should at least try," he says, stripping off his pants. I pull his shirt over my head and dive onto the mattress.

We don't make it through the floor, but not for lack of trying. Javi is very thorough and by the time we both fall into an exhausted sleep I've been fucked so hard and so much I can't see a reason for ever leaving this bed. Mattress. Whatever.

Chapter Twelve

'm disoriented when I wake up, roll over, and find myself at eye level with the bottom drawer of my dresser. Then memories of the previous night come flooding back to me and I wince. I've definitely got some road rash down low, but it's a good kind of pain. Used hard and used good.

Javi enters my room in fresh clothes and his hair is wet.

"Hey," I say, grinning up at him. "You owe me a bedframe."

He crouches down and gives me a kiss before sitting on the mattress next to me.

"You more than earned it, Haze." The way he looks at me, like he wants to take off his clothes and start all over again makes me want to rip his shirt off. "But how about some breakfast first?"

"Sure. Just let me take a shower."

He nods.

"Jett and Shannon headed back to our place so it's all yours. I bumped into them earlier and I bet Shannon is going to talk to your ear off about last night." As she does.

"Great. It's going to be fun explaining." Eh, she'll probably be fine with it. Javi and I were inevitable. She knew that.

I get up and grab some clothes out of my dresser and start walking toward the bathroom, but Javi stops me.

"Is there a reason you need to wear clothes? You look so much better like this."

His eyes roam up and down my body and I almost blush. No one's ever looked at me quite like that. Usually they see my tits and don't go any further. But Javi looks at everything, including my face.

"Because I don't want to get arrested for indecent exposure," I say, backing up.

"Oh, it would definitely be decent exposure," he says as I open the door and then shut it behind me. Oh, Javi.

We get breakfast at Hank's again and then Javi drops me off right in front of my first class, giving me a searing kiss before shoving me out the door.

The kiss makes me want to get back into the truck, but I don't. I walk away slowly, making sure I put my hips into it. I look at him over my shoulder and give him a wink. He whistles and then drives off.

He's there when I'm done with class, waiting patiently in his truck. And he's reading. As if I needed one more reason to fuck him senseless.

"Whatcha reading?" I say as I slide in. He gives me a kiss hello and then goes back to his book, holding up one finger.

A minute later he puts a folded piece of paper in the book to mark his place and sets it on the seat between us.

"Just something for class. How was your day? I must say that driving you around is quite enjoyable." I kind of like it too, but it can't be a permanent thing. He's not my boyfriend.

"Well, you did break my bed." I'm going to milk that for all it's worth and then milk it a little more to make sure I've gotten everything out of it that I can.

"Okay, okay," he says, putting his hands up and turning the truck on. "Where do you want to get a new one? There's some furniture stores out by the mall in Hartford." I just figured we'd go to Salvation Army or something, but if he wants to fork out money for a brand new bed, who am I to stop him?

"You don't have to spend a lot. I'm really not picky."

He waves that off.

"It's no big. Bedframes aren't that expensive. Do you want something like you had, or do you want something different?" I hadn't even though of that.

"I have no idea." Honest truth: I've never had new furniture. I've never even picked out furniture. I've always taken whatever I was given, or whatever I could find at a yard sale or junk store.

"Well, start thinking." He turns on the radio and flips to the classic rock station. I don't mind since sometimes they play the stuff I listen to.

"Do you have enough money?" I ask, cringing. I hate talking about money. It's one of the reasons Shannon and I work so well together. We both come from the same circumstances, so we understand how the other feels about finances without even having to ask.

Javi glances over at me.

"Don't even worry about it. I've got you covered." I was all excited about this bed thing and now I'm not. Every time I look at this bed, I'm going to think about Javi and how he bought it for me and it's probably going to make me feel like shit. Great. I never should have said it. But it was the heat of the moment. I'm not responsible for anything I say mid-orgasm.

"Are you sure?" I don't want to beat a dead horse, but I really don't want him to go into debt over me.

"Don't worry about it, Haze." He reaches out and squeezes my hand. I don't know whether to believe him or not, so I'm silent for the rest of the trip to the furniture store.

Javi parks in front of one of those warehouse places with so much furniture you could furnish a small country with the contents.

"You should be able to find something here, but if not, we have options." He points down the street and there's a strip of such furniture stores. How they can all stay in business is beyond me, but the parking lots are full and people are busy strapping mattresses and couches onto the tops of their vehicles.

"Okay," I say and follow Javi into the place.

It's fucking massive and packed with everything you could need for a home. He heads right for the bedframes in the back and I walk behind him, a bit overwhelmed by everything.

"Okay, here you go. I'll just be here," he says, sitting in a nearby recliner and popping out the footrest.

I give him a look.

"Go, browse. I'll be here if you need me." He leans back like he's hanging out in his own home and watching a big game. He's strange sometimes.

I walk up and down the rows of bedframes that are all set up with naked mattresses. There are a lot of choices and most of them, I think, are pretty ugly. My old frame had been functional and that was about it. If I have the chance to get something I actually like, I'm going to take it. I find a white iron frame that's kind of pretty, but the price is ridiculous. I start looking at the other prices and cringing. I can't make Javi pay for this. Hell, he's pretty much buying all my groceries as it is.

I check price before I check anything else and finally find a simple wooden frame that's the cheapest. It looks almost exactly like my old one. I go back to where Javi was sitting and find him in another chair, several rows of recliners away.

"I've been testing the chairs. Only way to know which one you want is by sitting in every single one. You find something?" He gets up with a groan. Must have been a comfortable chair.

"Yup," I say and lead him over to it.

"You want this one?" I nod. Javi walks around it and looks at the price.

"This doesn't say 'Hazel' to me. But if this is what you want, this is what you want. I would have thought you'd go for something like that." He points at a frame I would choose if I was the one buying and had plenty of money. It's more of a platform, black with a leather-covered headboard. Sleek and modern and cool. The fact that Javi picked out the one I ultimately want kind of freaks me out.

"That one's really expensive," I say, my face red. Javi goes over to it and looks at the tag.

"Nah, it's on sale. See?" He holds up the red tag that says SALE. Still. The "sale" is a lot of money.

A salesperson in a polo shirt with the store's logo on it decides to come over and ask if we need any help. Javi jumps right in and asks her if the sale price on the fancy frame is the best they can do. The woman gives him a look and then they start talking. Haggling would be a better term.

I walk over and grab his arm, trying to make him stop, but he won't. The woman finally caves and goes to ask her manager if she can give an additional ten percent off.

Javi grins at me as if he's won the lottery.

"Never underestimate my ability to haggle."

"What are you doing? I didn't say I wanted that one."

He puts his arm around me.

"You didn't have to. I just knew."

I open my mouth to argue and he just kisses me.

That shuts me up.

After his victory with the bedframe, Javi is on a roll. It's almost like he's possessed. He talks me into a new lamp, an extra chair for our kitchen table, which will bring the number of chairs to an even four, and he almost talks me into a new dresser, but I draw the line.

"Why are you doing this?"

He does that one shoulder shrug that drives me up a wall.

"Because I want to. Why is it crazy for someone to want to do something nice for you?" Doing something nice isn't crazy. Buying a bedframe and an entire living room set for someone is crazy.

"Well, considering this might look like payment for last night, yes, it is crazy." Javi glares at me.

"This has nothing to do with last night. I mean, other than the fact that your bed broke. The rest of this is just because I want to. Shit, Haze. Kick a guy for trying." He's trying to turn this around and make me look like I'm ungrateful and I don't like it.

"Hey," I say, jabbing my finger into his chest. "I didn't ask you to do this. Yes, I said something about the bedframe, but I didn't ask for the most expensive one in the store, or for anything else. I don't want anything from you, Javi. I just want… I just want…" I can't put it into words.

He sighs.

"I know, I know. You didn't ask for it, but you're getting it. Because I want to. I like the idea of you sleeping in a bed I bought for you. I really like the idea of having sex with you in a bed I bought for you. If that makes me a jerk, fine. I'll live with that. But I want to give you what you want. I can't explain it, I just do. I'm not trying to make any sort of political statement. You want this thing and I'm happy to give it to you. That's it." He holds out his hands and then drops them to his sides.

I can't seem to make him see what the bed represents to me. Why it's not okay for him to spend this much money. But explaining that would require me to tell him about my past and growing up and I don't think I can do that. So the price for me not telling him is letting him buy me the damn bed. And a lamp. And a chair.

"Fine," I say. "Fine. And I'm not trying to be ungrateful. Because I'm not. This is… this is a lot, Javi. Thank you." He puts his arms around me and holds me close in the middle of the furniture store.

"You're welcome, Haze."

Because he refused to pay a delivery fee, we head to the back of the warehouse and Javi and a few of the guys who work at the store load everything into his truck.

"How in the hell are you going to get that into my room?" I ask, realizing the bed is going to be bigger than my previous one.

"It'll work. We might need to move some things around, but it will work. Trust me." I'm going to have to take his word for it, because I don't see how this is going to work. Maybe if the bed doesn't fit I can convince him to take it back and get the cheap one.

"What the hell?" Shannon says when we walk through the door, me carrying the lamp, and Javi with the chair.

"We went furniture shopping," I say as I take the lamp into my bedroom. The old frame is gone.

"Where did my bed go?" Jett shoves his hands in his pockets and Shannon pretends to look innocent.

"We got it out of the way. Javi called and said you'd be bringing in something new so you'd need the old one out of there. It's now resting peacefully in the Dumpster," Shannon says. "That was brilliant, by the way. Breaking your bed to get a new one. I should try that."

"You can have mine, princess," Jett says. "I'd be happy to bring it here." Shannon shoots him a look and he doesn't say anything else.

Huh. Looks like there's some tension at the mention of Jett moving his things here. I mean, it does seem silly that they both pay rent at two places when they practically live together now. But I've decided to stay out of Shannon's relationships. Look how much good I did last time I meddled. It's a miracle Shannon is still speaking to me, let a alone living with me.

We all head back down to Javi's truck and what ensues is very reminiscent of the *FRIENDS* episode where they try to move a couch. Only Shannon and I are the ones who keep yelling "PIVOT!" Jett and Javi don't find it as hilarious as we do.

"We don't need to pivot!" Javi yells and I just stick my tongue out at him. We finally get the base of the frame into my room and miracle of miracles, it does actually fit. Guess I underestimated the dimensions of my bedroom. Javi puts the rest together with the help of some tools he has stashed in his truck and then it's time for the mattress.

"Very cool, Haze," Shannon says once it's all together and the bed is made. My sheets don't exactly match, but oh well.

"We should have gotten you some new sheets," Javi says and I glare at him. Since when did he become the decorating police?

"Well, I think we're going to order dinner tonight," Shannon says and takes our orders for pizza before she and Jett leave Javi and me alone with the new bed.

"What do you think?" Javi asks, sitting down on the edge of the bed and patting the space next to him. I sit down and we both lie back and stare at the ceiling.

"It's really nice, Javi. I don't know how I can ever thank you." He turns his head to the side and I do as well. We're close enough to kiss.

"I can think of a few ways," he says, wiggling his eyebrows.

"Ugh, you're disgusting."

"You like it." I sigh.

"Yeah, I do."

He puts his hand under my chin and pulls my face close for a kiss.

"I like you too," he says.

We kiss a little and then he puts his arm around me and I snuggle close.

"What do you say we should try and break this one tonight?" I say and he chuckles.

"I like this plan, and I think I'm more than up to the challenge."

Chapter Thirteen

The bed doesn't break. Not that night and not the next. Finally, it's Friday night and everyone's decided to go out. Unfortunately I picked up an extra shift at the bar, so I'm out of luck.

"What are you going to do?" I ask Javi that evening as he watches me getting ready for work. I didn't ask him about his plans earlier, since I figured he had some.

"I fancy a drink and my favorite bartender is working tonight." I turn around and pull my shirt into place.

"You mean you're going to come and pester me while I'm working." He gets up.

"'Pester' is such a harsh word. I think of it more as keeping you company. But if you don't want me there, I can make alternate plans. I don't want you to feel like you have to put up with me *all* the time." In truth, I like having Javi around, but it'd hard to go from only seeing someone a few times a week to seeing them all the time. You can't make an adjustment that fast.

"It's not that I don't want to see you, I do…" I start to say, but he stops me.

"You don't have to explain at all. If you ever need some time for just you, let me know. I know I have a tendency to just shove myself into a situation and ask questions after." I snort.

"Well, that's good to know. Yes, I think I'd just like to go to work. Besides, you can be very distracting and I don't think my boss would like it if I was caught banging you in the break room." The thought has crossed my mind, but I need the money more than the sex.

"Pity," Javi says, lifting my shirt and letting his fingers flutter over my exposed stomach. "But I have things to do. Oh, don't give me that look." I'm not giving him any look, as far as I know.

"I'm not going out to have sex with someone else. I'll just go home, do some laundry, homework, that sort of thing. It's no big." I didn't say he was going out with someone else. But the idea of him doing so sends a flare of a highly unpleasant emotion surging through me.

Jealousy.

Normally, I think of myself as the kind of girl who doesn't get jealous. But that's usually due to the fact that I don't do committed relationships. Flings never involve jealousy since they are just that. Flings. Casual sex.

This thing with Javi... it started out different and continues to be different.

"You can do what you want. We're only together-ish. I have no claim on your time. You can come and go as you please and see who you want." I say the words, but they feel empty. I don't want him to do any of those things. I want him to come to work with me and sit at the bar and make sexual jokes and irritate me.

"That's sweet, but I'd rather just be alone if I can't be with you." And then he slaps my ass. "Make good money, gorgeous."

He heads out the door and calls goodbye to Jett and Shannon, Daisy and Jordyn, who are here early.

I shake myself, trying to shake off all my annoying feelings and go back to fixing my hair.

Work is awful. Either there's a full moon, or all the assholes decided to get together and venture out at the same time.

I get a drink spilled down my back, my ass grabbed and plenty of propositions I wouldn't take if they gave me a billion dollars.

I'm irritable and missing Javi.

No, I'm not missing Javi. I just fucking saw him. I can spend a few hours away from him. I'm not a clingy girl who has no identity when she's not with her man. Hell, he's not even my man. He's a man I have sex with. That's it.

I'm an independent woman and I can take care of myself.

"Rough night?" Regina, one of the other regular bartenders asks as I slam some cash into the register.

"You could say that. It's like we have a blinking sign that says 'Assholes Drink Here' or something." She pats my shoulder.

"Cheer up. Have a shot. We only have a few more hours." That actually doesn't sound like a bad idea. I pour myself a small whiskey shot and down it. The burn down my throat is wonderful and the alcohol gives me a warm feeling as soon as it hits my bloodstream. It won't stop people from being jerks, but it makes me care about them less.

By the end of the night, I'm dreading coming in tomorrow (which is technically today) if it's going to be as bad as tonight. But I'll suck it up. I've had much worse nights before.

I say farewell to my comrades and head to my car. I'd changed my shirt when one had gotten soaked with beer, but I didn't have an extra pair of pants. I make a note to bring an entire new outfit with me next time.

The shower is my only destination when I got home. I don't even stop in my bedroom to get extra clothes. The place is dark aside from the light in the kitchen Shannon had left on for me so I wouldn't have to fumble for the switch.

I drop my clothes on the floor and turn the setting on as hot as it goes. Even my underwear hasn't escaped the beer attack and sticks to my skin. Gross.

The scalding spray pounds down on me as I close my eyes and tilt my face up. I'm so tired and distracted that I don't even hear the door open.

"Knock, knock," a male voice says and I scream. "Relax, it's just me." Javi pulls aside the shower curtain and then steps in with me. He's naked, so he must have taken his clothes off before he spoke.

"What are you doing here?" I say, holding my hand to my heart. "You scared the shit out of me! Haven't you even seen *Psycho*?" I whack him a few times, but he just wraps his arms around me.

"Easy there. I went home and did some stuff and then figured I'd wait here for you to come home. I got a lot of homework done, by the way. Your place is much more conducive to studying. No idea why." He puts a kiss on my cheek and lets me go.

"You can't just sneak up on a girl in the shower." I cross my arms. He just grabs the bottle of shampoo.

"Here, let me wash your hair to make up for scaring you."

"Javi."

"What?"

"Next time, text me and tell me you're going to be here and knock on the actual door before you get in the shower with me. Seriously." He nods and pops the top of the bottle.

"Text and knock. Got it. Turn around and tilt your head back." I do as he asks and he starts washing my hair.

"How was work?"

"Terrible. Someone spilled beer all over me. I had an extra shirt, but I forgot to bring pants so I was sticky all night. And there were some real charmers." Javi moves his fingers in my scalp, working the shampoo into a lather and massaging at the same time. It feels really good. The last time I remember anyone else washing my hair, I was probably a kid and my mom did it.

"See? I should have been there. I would have taught them some manners and how to treat a woman who is serving you." I snort.

"Yeah, I'm sure you could have given them etiquette lessons, Javier."

"I'm a total gentleman," he says with shock. I turn my head and he winks at me. "Remember that time when I opened a door for you? And that time I bought you a bed?"

"After you broke the other one," I say, but I'm laughing. The tension of the night melts from my shoulders as Javi rinses the shampoo out of my hair, being careful not to let any of it get in my eyes.

"I think we were both responsible for the bed breaking. I told you it was going to be rough and you gave me the green light to go ahead." I turn around and smack him across the chest. "Plus, that was a really weak bedframe. You should have invested in something sturdier if you were going to enjoy those sorts of activities on it." I grab my loofah and start beating him with it and he pretends to cower in the corner.

We're both laughing as he grabs me around the waist and dunks me under the spray.

"Hey!" I yell and then we wrestle for a little while, getting water everywhere.

When we finally call a truce, I wash Javi's hair and then we condition together before washing each other thoroughly and finally shutting off the water.

He grabs a towel and wraps me in it before getting one for himself. Then he throws me over his shoulder and carries me to the bedroom where he throws me down on the bed and we do the opposite of getting clean. We get dirty.

Javi is still sleeping when I wake up early the next morning, so I get up to have breakfast with Shannon.

"How's the, uh, new bed working out?" Shannon asks when she comes home from Jett's. I feel like I haven't seen her without Jett or Javi present in ages. We've both been preoccupied.

"It's holding up," I say and she giggles.

"And how are other things going? I know you don't really want to talk about it, but I'm dying here. I need some details. Not *those* kind of details, but just some... other details. You're killing me." She leans her head on her hands and begs.

"Well, there aren't a whole lot of details. Javi and I aren't together like boyfriend and girlfriend, but we're seeing each other, I guess. And sleeping with each other. But it's not exclusive and it's not anything permanent. It's just sort of a 'for now' kind of thing. And if something changes, that'll be fine. We're just having fun together." That's the best way I can put it.

Shannon looks at me for a long time.

"And you're fine with the casual thing? Because I've seen the way you look at him. And the way he looks at you. And how you are together and that doesn't seem like a casual thing. He's practically living here." I'm not going to point out that she's practically living with Jett. It's a bit of a pot calling the kettle black situation.

"He just sleeps here. With me. You've seen their place. It's awful. Our place might not be great, but it's better than theirs," I say. This is an undisputable fact.

Shannon makes a face at the mention of Javi and Jett's apartment.

"I keep telling Jett to get a better place, but it's not easy. The good places are so expensive and the bad places are cheap but... bad."

Landlords know students are desperate, so they rent apartments that no one else would be caught dead living in and pocket the cash. Pretty sweet deal when you think about it.

"They just have no money," she says.

"Well, I don't know about Jett's situation, but Javi seems to have no problem. He paid for the bed and he's been buying groceries and all sorts of stuff. And I'm positive he doesn't have a job because he never has to go to work, but he still seems to have money." Shannon is the only one I can talk to about this. If I ask Javi, he'd probably just make a joke or something. Besides, I hate talking about money with him.

"Weird. Maybe he's got a scholarship or something? Some people take out more student loans than they need so they have money to live on. Maybe he's doing that." I've heard of people doing that, but I didn't think you'd get enough student loan money to pay rent and go out and buy expensive bedframes and truffles with. There has to be another explanation.

"I don't know what it is, but I really want to. It's driving me nuts."

"Just ask him." I get up and make some more coffee. I'm going to need more than a few cups today. Last night was brutal.

"I can't. That's the kind of thing I can't ask. If I was a girlfriend, maybe. But it's really none of my business. We nearly had a fight over the bedframe. I'd rather not go there if I can help it." Shannon sighs and I sit back down to wait for the coffee to percolate.

"That's a tough one. I guess you could maybe ask a simple question when you're out. Something that's not too prying." I've thought about that.

"Anyway, enough about me. How are you doing?" She smiles and tilts her head down.

"Good. Really good. Jett is just so…" she waves one hand, looking for a way to describe him.

"Awesome? Perfect for you?" I supply. She grins wider.

"I just can't believe we got so lucky. I mean, if I hadn't been at that café on that day and he hadn't asked me to watch his computer and then you hadn't been annoying me about turning in my V card then it might never have happened." By that logic, if Shannon and Jett hadn't gotten together, I might never have met Javier.

Was there such a thing as fate? Or was it just chance that ruled your life? Both were sobering thoughts that I didn't like to dwell too much on.

"I'm glad you're happy and that everything worked out. I'm still sorry for being so awful to you. You know that, right?" I feel like I'm constantly apologizing, but I still feel terrible about it. What I had done was really shitty.

"It's okay. I should have stood up for myself. We were both in the wrong. But it's better now and everything's okay." She gets up and pours coffee into her cup and then I hand her mine.

"So, do you think this thing with Javier will get serious? As in calling him your boyfriend?" Ugh, I thought we were done with me. I don't want to talk about me anymore.

She hands me my coffee and I burn my mouth on the first sip.

"I don't know, Shan. I'm just taking it as it comes and living each day and all that shit. I just don't know."

"Don't know what?" Javi's voice says and I turn to see him shuffling into the kitchen, his hair all over the place and his eyes a little puffy. He looks adorable and I just want to climb back into bed and cuddle with him for the rest of the day.

"Nothing. Good morning, sleepyhead," I say as he crashes down in the new chair. "Did you not sleep?"

"No, I did, after you got back. But staying up waiting for you wasn't easy. I don't know how you work so late and then have the energy to get up in the morning." I don't either. Coffee, I guess. And energy shots when I'm working.

"Coffee?" Shannon says and he nods.

"Please."

She gives him a cup and sits back down.

"Well, I should get going. Jett and I are heading to the library to get a bunch of work done. Have a good night at work." She gets up and leaves. It's just Javi and me.

"You didn't have to wait up for me," I say, going to the fridge. It's well-stocked, thanks to him. I pull out some eggs and butter and grab some bread from the box on the counter.

"I know. But it just sort of happened. What are you doing?"

"I'm making eggs and toast. I can do it, I promise. Just sit and drink your coffee and wake up." I grab a spatula and brandish it at him so he won't jump up and start helping me. I can cook some eggs and make some toast. I mean, I can now that Javi taught me how.

He's pressing his lips together like he really wants to comment on my egg-making abilities, but I just glare at him.

"Not one word. I can do this." He nods and keeps his mouth shut the whole time I scramble the eggs with just a little bit of milk and pour them in the pan with the butter and then add salt and pepper and work them around so they cook, but not so much they get stiff.

"See?" I say when the eggs are done. He gets up and pulls some plates down and I spoon out some of the eggs and two pieces of toast on his plate. Javi always eats his eggs with hot sauce, so it's already on the table and waiting for him.

I have my eggs with ketchup and plenty of salt. Javi takes a bite and nods in appreciation.

"Good."

"Told you I could do it." I take a bite myself and they are good. Not as good as when Javi makes them, though. He's just got the magic touch when it comes to food. I could make the exact same thing with the exact same ingredients and it still wouldn't taste the same as when he makes it.

"I have full faith in your cooking abilities," he says, but it looks like it almost physically hurts him to admit that.

"You're such a liar. But it's okay. I like you anyway." We smile at each other over our steaming plates of eggs and there's a moment. One of those moments where time slows down and you feel so happy that it expands in your chest and you're afraid you might explode or die from it.

I break the moment by looking down at my plate. Sometimes being with Javi is too much.

"So, what are you up to today?" It's a stupid question and I hate the way it comes out of my mouth.

"Well, homework and then I thought maybe we could go do something fun. I mean, something that doesn't require a condom." I nearly choke on my eggs.

"You mean like a date?" I ask.

He does the one shoulder shrug.

"Sure, if you want to call it that. But since we aren't technically dating, it wouldn't be a date. Just two people going to the same place together at the same time." It sounds so much less romantic like that.

"Oh. Well, what did you have in mind?"

"Not sure. I was hoping to get your input. I'm not really used to taking girls out during the day." I roll my eyes, but it's true. Javi isn't the date guy. He isn't the one who would take you to the fair and hold your hand and buy you cotton candy. He's the guy you bring home from the bar, have sex with and never call again. Not me, obviously, but he might have been if I hadn't gotten to know him first.

"Um, I'm not sure," I say. I too have not been on an actual day date in forever. What do people even do on day dates? I don't want to go bowling or do anything athletic. And I sure as hell don't want to participate in any sort of collegiate activities like a game or something.

"Think about it and let me know."

"Will do." We finish our eggs and do the dishes together and then hit the books.

"How much do you have?" he asks. I glance at the clock on the DVD player.

"Enough to work through lunch." I have a research paper due next week that is going to require a lot of sources that I still need to find, both online and from books.

"Good, me too."

And that's the end of the talking for the next several hours. Both of us are engrossed with our work. It's a lot easier now to work with Javi than it was the first time. He's much less distracting now that I know I can have sex with him after all my work is done. Reward system, you know?

When I finally get all my sources and finish my reading for my other classes, I close my books and stretch.

"You done?" Javi asks. Clearly, he's still got stuff to do.

"Yeah, but if you still need to work, that's fine. I can go in my room or something." He shakes his head.

"No, it's fine. Do whatever you want. I can focus through a hurricane." I smile slowly.

"That sounds like a challenge." He looks up from his books.

"Hazel."

"What?" I say innocently. "You were the one who brought it up."

He narrows his eyes.

"Fine, fine. But you're cool if I watch TV?" He nods once and goes back to his reading. I turn on the TV and start flipping through the channels, looking for something that isn't crap. It's not easy.

I like reality TV as much as the next person, but this new trend of reality shows where people are doing stupid things while naked has got to stop. Besides, they blur everything out, so what's the point?

I finally settle on a marathon of *Gilmore Girls*. You can't go wrong with that show, even though they talk so fast and there's no way someone would be that witty and have comebacks all the time. I've had a crush on Luke, the guy who owns the diner since I was a teenager.

I chuckle at some of my favorite bits, but Javi doesn't look up. Not even when two of the characters have a screaming fight as they are wont to do when things get tense.

He really does have intense concentration.

It's totally mean, but I decide to test him. I yawn and stretch my arms up high, letting my shirt ride up and show my stomach. Nothing. No reaction.

So then I stand up and start twisting from side to side, like I'm working a kink out of my back. Nada. It's time for drastic measures.

I thrust my chest out and stretch back until my spine pops. I glance down at Javi and he's still reading his books.

Then I just take my shirt off. I'm not wearing a bra, so I'm completely topless.

His eyes are still scanning across the page just as fast as before.

I take my pants off so I'm just in my panties and stand right in front of him.

"You're really pulling out all the stops, aren't you?" he says, his head tilted down as he turns the page of his book.

"I am practically naked here and you won't even look up. Okay, you win. I was just about to start getting myself off to see if you'd get distracted by that."

"What?" he says, looking up.

"Ha!" I clap my hands once in triumph. "Made you look."

"Oh, you are naked," he says, looking me up and down. "I could tell you were doing something, but I was doing my best to ignore it. Now I can't." He puts his books aside and gets up.

"You have an incredible body, Haze." His hands skim my sides. Every time he touches me, it turns me on. It doesn't matter if it's a quick touch, just to pass me a cup of coffee or hand me something. Everything he does makes me want him.

"You wanna go back to studying?" I say, stepping closer as his hands become more adventurous.

"I really should. But I suppose it can wait for a little while."

"A little while? You planning on being a two pump chump?" He bursts out laughing.

"Gorgeous, I'm never a two pump chump. Let me show you." He leads me to the bedroom and shows me that yes, he can go the distance. Twice.

Later, we go back out to the living room and lie on the couch together. He's just wearing his boxers and I have his shirt on. I can tell he likes it when I wear his shirt and nothing else. I like it too.

"So, this woman is her mother? She doesn't look old enough to have a teen daughter," Javi says, commenting on the *Gilmore Girls* marathon. I'm surprised he's actually watching it.

"She had Rory when she was sixteen."

"Oh, got it. What's with the guy and the baseball cap?" He points at the screen.

"That's Luke. He owns the diner and he's in love with Lorelai but he doesn't know it yet."

"Ah! Spoiler alert. Now you've totally ruined the show for me. Thanks a lot." He pretends to be mad, but I just poke him in the stomach.

"You'll get over it. Besides, their first kiss doesn't happen for two more seasons. They drew it out, the bastards."

"Those bastards," Javi says, shaking his fist at the screen.

"Don't make fun of me, I love this show."

He kisses my forehead.

"I'm not making fun. Not at all."

I sit up, realizing something.

"Hey, weren't we supposed to go out on a date, or something?" I completely forgot about it. Sex can make you forget about just about everything.

"Right. Do you still want to go?" He starts to get up, but I put my hand on his chest to stop him.

"Honestly? No. I'm cool with just this and then ordering something and getting it delivered. Then only one of us has to get dressed."

Javi hugs me tight.

"I love the way your mind works, Hazel. *Gilmore Girls* and takeout it is."

Chapter Fourteen

I hesitate that night before I go to work. Javi says he's going to finish the homework I interrupted today, and I'm totally okay with that. But part of me wants to ask him to come to work with me.

A larger part screams that asking him to come is ridiculous and needy and unnecessary. So I don't ask him.

Tonight is much better than last night, thank God. The customers seem to be more polite and they're much better tippers. I even have a nice conversation with a guy who's just passing through and needs a beer before he's on his way. I love talking to strangers (nice, interesting strangers), which is probably one of the reasons I enjoy working at the bar. At least on most nights.

I'm in a much better mood when I come back to the apartment and I don't freak when I find Javi waiting for me in the living room, with only the glow of the TV as a light.

"What are you watching?" I ask as I pull off my shoes and drop my bag on the floor. I see the screen and hear the voices and stare at Javi in shock.

"You're still watching *Gilmore Girls*? How many hours has it been?" I sit next to him on the couch and he gives me a kiss hello.

"This is all your fault. When they say marathon, they mean it. It's all Gilmores all the time for two weeks." It's sad how I don't even need to see the title of the episode to know what's going to happen.

"So you like it? I mean, most people don't spend hours watching a show that they hate."

"I don't know what happened. I was watching it with you and the next thing I know I'm screaming at the screen for Luke and Lorelai to kiss." He looks a little bewildered. And tired.

"You've been Gilmored. It's okay, it happens to the best of us. How about you join me in the shower and we can talk about Luke and Lorelai and why Dean was a terrible boyfriend for Rory." He just nods and I lead him into the bathroom. He's still mumbling about *Gilmore Girls* when I shove him into bed.

I just laugh and turn out the light.

Despite not being a couple, Javi and I settle into a sort of routine. He stays nights with me, but we drive separately to classes during the day. He understands my need to be independent.

Sometimes I get back from class and he's still at his place, but he always shows up for dinner which we share with Shannon and Jett most nights and then there's sex and sleeping.

The sex is more than awesome and the new bed gets quite a workout, but it's the other things I really like. I adore knowing that someone will be there during dinner to talk to about my day, other than Shannon. I adore waking up in the middle of the night and hearing someone else sleeping in the same room.

I had no idea how lonely I was before Javi started coming over. Sure, I told myself I didn't need the strings and complications of a relationship and I didn't want anyone in my personal space all the time.

But now that I'm doing this thing with Javi, it's all I want. I want him here, all the time, with me.

I want to go to sleep with him and wake up and eat breakfast with him. I want him to wait for me in his truck and pick me up after classes. I want him to hold my hand and shop for groceries and all that domestic crap. I want the things with him I told myself I never, ever, wanted and now they're all I can think about.

I want to share my life with him. All of it. Every moment. I mean, I still don't know how I feel about marriage, but I could imagine being married to Javi.

It wouldn't be a typical marriage, that's for damn sure.

"Taste," Javi says one night when he's making some sort of complicated sauce that I'm pretty sure he stole from the Julia Child cookbook. I caught him reading it the other day and I've been joking about him starting a blog and testing all the recipes. He thought it was funny the first three times I mentioned it. Now, not so much.

He blows on the sauce in the spoon and then lifts it to my mouth. I sip a little and I nearly fall over.

"I have no idea what that is, but I want you to make enough so I can fill the bathtub and go swimming in it."

"I'll take that as a ringing endorsement," he says, licking the rest of the sauce off the spoon and then washing it in the sink. For someone who's pretty messy, Javi is a neat freak when he cooks. It doesn't make any sense.

I've noticed he's much less of a slob at my place than he is at his. Feeling guilty that he always has to come over here, I've agreed to go over to his place for a few hours at a time. It's much better now that Shannon has been staying there. The weird smell that I suspect was mold is gone, and they finally got rid of the nasty, nasty couch and got something better.

"What's cookin'?" Jett says as he walks in the door.

"Coq au vin," Javi says and I snort with laughter.

"What? You said cock. I can't help it if that word always makes me laugh." Javi glares at me. He always gets super serious when he cooks and doesn't appreciate my jokes as much. Kind of kills the fun.

"No, I said coq. As in the French word for chicken. Chicken with a wine sauce. That's what we're having. With mushrooms and potatoes and Shannon's going to make a salad and then we've got ice cream for dessert. I wanted to make Boeuf Bourguignon, but it takes more than an hour to cook, so I went with something that's quicker." I gotta say, hearing Javi pronounce the French words definitely turns me on. He has an excellent accent.

"Have you ever studied French?" I ask, putting my hand on his shoulder and leaning into him.

"A little. And some Spanish and Italian and Greek."

"In your spare time?" Javi is so much smarter than I ever knew. I have no idea why he hides it. Or, that's not really it. I guess he's just not as open about it as I would expect him to be. Maybe that's one of the reasons I like him so much. He doesn't throw his intelligence in other people's faces.

"I had a lot more time before you came along," he says.

"Yeah, me too."

"What did you do with your time?" he asks. Studied more. Worked more hours at the bar. Definitely watched more television. Nothing super important. Javi hasn't taken up any time I wasn't willing to give him.

"Not much. I'd rather hang out with you."

Jett goes to the fridge and pulls out a soda and starts asking Javi about something.

Shannon comes in.

"Sorry! Sorry. I got tied up at work." Jett gives her a kiss and she heads to her bedroom to get her work clothes off. Even though she works in the Operations department of the bank, she still has to dress nicely. And she likes it anyway. One of the reasons she wants to work in a big shiny office building is so she can wear sexy pumps and suits and pencil skirts every day. I can't say anything, because I'm going to be wearing similar outfits as a lawyer.

I still don't know what Javi wants to be. He and I don't talk about that kind of thing. We don't talk about the future further than the next week. There's something freeing in that, but it's stressful, too. Now that I'm in this, I want to know how long it's going to last. Is Javi going to get tired of me? We haven't even had a huge fight yet, so I don't know if the first one is going to trigger the end of being together-ish.

I'm one giant ball of confusion.

Chapter Fifteen

Javi has another one of his sullen days the next week. It's like he just shuts down and won't respond to anything I say or do. I might as well be talking to a wall.

"What the fuck is wrong with you?" I finally say as we're lying in bed. I've been trying to seduce him, but it isn't working.

"Nothing. I'm fine."

"Bullshit, Javier. You're being weird and sullen and if you're going to be weird and sullen with me, I'd like to know why and then you can go back to being weird and sullen and I'll just read a book." I turn on my side and glare at him. He's on his back, looking up at the ceiling.

"You're not my girlfriend. You don't have to listen to me bitch about my feelings." True, but that doesn't mean I don't care.

"Cut it out. You're in my house and you're being a jerk. If you don't want to be here, then go home. Or tell me what it is. Get it off your chest so it will stop annoying both of us." My voice is getting louder and I'm getting more frustrated and I'm really glad Jett and Shannon are staying at his place so I can yell as loud as I want. The downstairs neighbors are drug dealers so they wouldn't call the cops on us even if the apartment was on fire.

"Fine, I'll leave." He starts to get out of bed, but I grab his arm and dig my nails in.

"You don't just get to run away. You don't get to do that. We might not be dating, but this is some sort of relationship." He jerks his arm out of my grasp.

"It's not your problem, Hazel. You don't have to fucking fix me. I'm not broken and I'm not your boyfriend and this is none of your business." This time when he tries to leave, I let him.

He doesn't want me tonight, and it's probably best to let him go. I'm not going to do battle with him.

"Fine. Leave." He looks back at me as he puts his clothes on and packs up his bag. There's a flash of something like pain across his face and then his features go blank as he walks out the door and slams it.

What. The. Fuck.

I can't get to sleep after Javi leaves. My new bed is large and empty without him and I can't get comfortable no matter how much tossing and turning I do.

After a while I give up, grab a blanket and head out to the living room and turn on the television. Maybe that will somehow distract my mind for a little while.

I'm flipping through the channels, not even caring what's on and then there's a knock at the door. Knowing who's going to be standing on the other side, I consider for a moment if I'm going to answer it. Javi almost never knocks.

I walk to the door and open it a few inches.

"Hey," he says. He looks like shit and smells like cigarettes.

"You smoked," I say and he nods.

"Can I come in?" His voice cracks a little and he shivers. It's a cold night and he's just wearing the t-shirt he left in.

"I don't know. Are you going to not be a jerk to me?" He nods slowly.

"I'm sorry. I'm having a bad day and I took it out on you. I shouldn't have done that and I'm sorry. I don't know if you've noticed this or not, but I'm not very good at sharing anything personal, other than when I want to sleep with you. There are a lot of things you don't know about me and I don't know if I'm ready to talk about them with you yet. I do know that I want to let you in. It's fucking cold out here." He wraps his arms around himself and I open the door wider.

"Come in, Javi." He comes in and I shut the door behind him. He has his bag with him and when I turn and head for my bedroom, he follows me.

"Thank you, Hazel. For letting me back in. I probably wouldn't have." I sigh and hold my bedroom door open for him.

"Yeah, well, you're not me. So," I say.

He cracks a tiny smile and then takes off his clothes and gets back into bed. I follow suit and he pulls me close.

"I want you to know about me, but I'm scared. You scare me. This scares me," he whispers in my ear. I turn in his arms so I'm facing him.

"I know. I'm scared too."

In the morning, Javi is quiet, but he's not sad like he was last night. He's thoughtful now.

"Can I expect a lot of those sorts of nights? Because I'd like to prepare for them if they're going to be a regular thing," I ask as he makes us waffles. I told him I wasn't hungry, but he's making them anyway. Jett and Shannon are having breakfast on campus since they slept late and have to rush to class.

"I'll try and let you know ahead of time. Oh, and I guess I owe you two dinners now." Right, the smoking. I'd forgotten about that with everything else.

"Yup, you do. So I guess that means we're going to dinner. Sounds like a date." I hate to call a spade a spade, but two people who are sleeping together eating a meal in public can't really be construed as anything but a date.

"That's right, that's right. So, where would you like to go? And when? It's all up to you," he says. I don't want it to be up to me. I hate choosing things like that.

"I'll look and see. Maybe we could go someplace out of town." Most of the local places cater to poor college students so it's mostly pizza and sandwiches, nothing fancy.

"I'm up for something fancy if it means you get to wear a pretty dress." Come to think of it, Javi has never seen me in a dress. And I'd sure as hell love to see him in dress pants and a button-down. Fuck, that would be hot. Why hadn't I thought about this sooner?

"I'm up for something fancy if it means you wear a dress shirt and dress pants," I say and he groans.

"I don't know about that, Haze. I don't even own either of those things." I call bullshit on that one.

"Nice try, but I've seen your closet."

He whirls around, waffles forgotten.

"When?"

"Um, when you were doing something in the kitchen and I said I had to get something out of your room. I looked in your closet so I know what's in there. I also know you have dress shoes. They looked brand new, too."

Javi points his spatula at me.

"Stay out of my closet," he says.

"Oh, like you've stayed out of mine?"

He looks down. Ha. I know he's gone through my closet.

"So, don't get mad at me for doing the same thing you did. Turnabout is fair play." Or something like that.

"You are trouble," Javi says, coming over and giving me a kiss. "And you should wear the black dress with the straps that cross in the back. It would look amazing on you." I nip at his bottom lip and he winces.

"Easy girl."

"That's for going through my closet. You'd better stay out of my dresser if you know what's good for you." I definitely have stuff in my dresser I don't want him messing around with and it isn't my socks.

"Well now I'm intrigued. You shouldn't have said that." He gives me a wicked grin.

"You are bad. I don't know why I ever got involved with you. Big mistake."

"Huge mistake," Javi says, bringing his mouth to mine again. "The hugest mistake you've ever seen." I roll my eyes but kiss him anyway.

"So, where are we going?" he asks as I plug the address into my phone and then set the phone in the cupholder so he can hear the directions.

"Just follow the robot lady. Unless she tells you to drive into the river, or oncoming traffic," I say as the robotic voice starts to tell us to turn right.

"I don't like this," he grumbles, but he turns right anyway.

"Well, you don't have to. You're the one who lit up and lost the bet." Before, I wasn't so sure about the whole going out to dinner thing, but now I'm definitely in favor of it.

Javi looks unbelievable. Like, off the charts sexy.

His white button down shirt has been ironed and his pants have creases in them. He's even wearing his dress shoes like I asked him to. Per his request, I'm wearing the black dress, but since it's cold I've got tights on under it and a cardigan over it. Before we left he made me flash him a view of my back and I'm sure he'll make me do more later.

Shannon and Jett don't exactly get the whole concept of the date that isn't a date, but Shannon gives me a look that says she doesn't believe me.

This isn't a date. It feels like a date, but it isn't.

Javi turns on the radio and I flip it to the retro station.

"You lost the bet," I say as Depeche Mode's "Just Can't Get Enough" plays. Javi groans, but I start singing along over him.

"I swear, I will never smoke again if this is what I have to go through," he yells over the music and then the GPS robot tells him to turn left. It's chaos in the truck, but it's our chaos.

I keep singing and Javi pretends to sing to himself.

"You love it," I say.

"I can definitely say I don't love it. Not at all. I'd rather forget that most of the music in the eighties happened. Scratch most of the 90s as well." He makes a face.

"You're so full of shit. I don't believe you."

The song ends and Dave Matthews Band comes on and Javi bitches even more. He can whine all he wants, but I'm not changing the radio station.

"This is payback for all those sexual comments," I yell as I turn the music up even higher so his speakers crackle with the beat of the bass.

"Hell! I'm in heeeeeellllllll!" Javi yells and pretends to smash his face on the steering wheel.

"Oh grow up. It's just a little music. Widen your horizons. It's good for you." He shakes his head and the GPS robot gives us more directions.

I enjoy the music the rest of the way to the restaurant, and Javi complains about every song. It's hilarious and I enjoy it so much more than I should.

"Destination in 100 feet," the cool, emotionless voice says.

Javi pulls into the parking lot of the restaurant and turns the truck off.

"So, is this it?" he asks.

"Yup. What do you think? They have a mix of French and American and their chef is world-renowned or something." He looks up at the building, which appears to be an old barn from the outside, but I'd seen the pictures of the inside, so I know how nice it is.

"Shall we?" I say. I'm not sure if he's going to open my door, so I open it myself as he hops out.

"I would have gotten that for you." I shrug as he comes over to my side and shuts the truck door for me.

"I didn't know if we were doing that. You know, since this isn't a date."

We should probably write some rules down or something. Shannon told me about her and Jett's rules for when they "fake dated" and it doesn't sound like a terrible idea.

Javi opens the door of the restaurant for me, and I go to the podium where a woman in a gorgeous dress and slicked back hair is waiting.

"Do you have a reservation?" she says after greeting us with a smile.

"Yes, it's under Cruz," I answer. I gave Javier's last name when I called to make the reservation.

His eyebrows go up in surprise. I shrug. I don't know why I gave his name.

The hostess finds the name on her list and grabs two menus before leading us to our table. Javier looks up at the beautiful ceiling, which is adorned with chandeliers made of old wagon wheels and twinkle lights. The floor is shiny, but clearly original with pock marks and divots everywhere. It's not exactly flat, so I have to be careful walking with my heels.

Our table is in a secluded corner. Very romantic.

"Someone will be right with you to get your drink orders." She gives us another smile and walks back to her station. The place is relatively quiet, which is nice. I'd picked a non-weekend night to come since I figured it would be less crowded.

"What do you think?" I ask as Javi scans the wine and spirits menu.

"It's nice. Really nice. I feel a little out of place, you know?" I do know. I feel the same way. Like the fancy police is going to bust their way in and throw us out for being impostors.

"Yup. But I wanted to take you to a place where you couldn't complain about the food." I grin at him and he sticks his tongue out.

"Wine is expensive, holy shit," he says under his breath. They have a few drink specials, but nothing that calls to me. I wonder if I can request something. Sometimes when it's slow in the winter at the bar, I create my own drinks with whatever's left over at the end of the night.

"It can be. What are you going to get?"

"Whatever's on tap," he says. Actually, a beer sounds good right now. Our waitress comes over and tells us about the specials and then asks what we want to drink. I don't know what half the food items she lists actually are, but I nod like I do. Javi probably does, so I can just ask him after she leaves. He orders a light beer and I get the same.

"Okay, so explain what all this stuff is," I whisper behind my menu after she leaves.

Javi chuckles and goes down the menu, pronouncing the French items so perfectly I want to drag him to the bathroom and have my way with him.

"Why are you staring at me?" he says. Shit, I've been staring at him.

"Um, because you were talking. It's polite to look at someone when they're speaking. I'm giving you my full attention." I set my menu down and prop my chin on my hands.

"No, you were staring at me with that look." He rests his arms on the table and leans forward.

"What look?"

"You know." He raises and lowers his eyebrows.

"Oh, please. I was looking at you because you were talking." I try to play it off like I wasn't staring at him like that.

"Say whatever you want, but you were looking at me like you wanted to forget all about dinner, pull me out back and go straight to dessert." The thought crossed my mind, but I would never do something like that.

"Whatever, Javi. I think you're imagining things." I pick up my menu and hide my face behind it.

"Oh, I wasn't imagining anything."

No, he wasn't.

I slip my shoe off and start dragging my foot up his pants leg. I can make this meal very uncomfortable for him if that's what he wants.

Javi's leg bangs against the table and he coughs. I slowly lower my menu and find him glaring at me.

"Evil. You are pure evil."

"You love it." He gets a serious look on his face, but it's gone in an instant. I remove my foot and slip my shoe back on. No one could see what I was doing since the tablecloths go all the way to the floor.

The waitress comes back with our beers and asks if we need some more time. I start to say yes, but then Javi speaks over me.

"No, we're ready to order." We are? I give him a look, but he just puts his hand up like "I got this." He orders a bunch of stuff, including an appetizer and entrée for me. And then hands the menu to the waitress. She takes mine and I give Javi a look.

"I thought this wasn't a date. Usually the guy orders for the girl when it's a date. But this isn't a date. I could have figured out what I wanted."

He shrugs one shoulder and now I'm picturing dragging him out to the Dumpster and beating him senseless.

"Sure, but I've been feeding you for a few weeks now. I know what you like and I know how much you love hearing me speak French. So there you go." Both of those things are true, but that doesn't mean I want him to order for me.

"Okay, for the next dinner, I get to order for myself. And you don't have to open the truck door for me. How's that?"

He nods.

"Seems fair. Or, I could open the truck door for you, and I can order for you."

"That's the exact opposite of what I just said."

"Is it?" He acts like he's thinking about it.

"Shut up, you know it is. I can order for myself, Javi."

"I know you can. I have no doubt in my mind that you can. But this is another one of those things I like to do." Ugh, here we go again.

"This isn't a bed, Javi." I sip my beer. It's perfectly cold and has just the right amount of foam. Their bartender really knows what they're doing.

"You're right. This is just ordering dinner. That's all."

"You're not my boyfriend," I say, feeling like a broken record. I can't remember how many times I've said that. But it bears repeating.

"I know," he says and he looks down into his beer glass. He seems disappointed this time when I say it.

"I think we should maybe make some rules for when we go out like this. You know, like Shannon and Jett had when they were together-but-not-together." He snorts.

"Yeah and look how well those rules worked out for them." He grins. Well, I didn't mean it to sound like that.

"Javi."

"Okay, okay. Should we maybe write these down? So we can remember them?" Javi has a fantastic memory. I know this for a fact, but it might be good to have something to refer to when he inevitably breaks whatever rules we're about to make. Because he will.

I pull out my phone and open an app that looks like a notepad so I can make a list.

"Okay, what's the first rule?" Javi asks.

"How about 'everyone opens their own car/truck doors'?"

Javi makes a sound of disapproval, but says "Fine."

"Second rule, Javi gets to order," he says. I kick at his leg under the table, but miss.

"This is all about give and take, Haze."

"Fine," I say and add it to the list. Javi wants to make the third rule about sex. Figures.

"Sex is not required but much appreciated," he says with a grin as he sips his beer. Where the hell is our food? It feels like we ordered it ages ago.

"I guess I can live with that," I say and add it to the list. "Any other rules you want to make about sex?"

"Too many to list."

"Moving on," I say to stop him from making this list hundreds of items long.

"What about paying? I mean, since you lost the bet you have to pay and next time you'll have to pay, but what about the other times?"

Javi drains his beer and sets the glass down.

"Other times?"

"Well, I mean, if there are other times. You know. Potentially." Great, now I'm talking about the future. That should be one of the rules. No future talk.

"I'm happy to pay any and all times we go out together. Unless you want to go Dutch." That could get expensive, but I don't want to seem like a mooch, so I write that any other time we go out that isn't bet related, we'll split the costs. I thought Javi would fight me on that one, but he lets it go.

Our appetizers arrive and it turns out to be goat cheese mixed with herbs, rolled into a ball with little dipping sauces.

"See? I told you to let me order for you," Javi says as I take a bite of one of the little cheese balls and nearly pass out.

"I hate that I love this," I say, my mouth full.

"I love that you hate that you love it." I give him a look and grab another cheese ball before he can eat them all. I end up eating nearly all of them. I can't help it. They're small and delicious and Javi doesn't move fast enough to grab them.

"I win," I say, nibbling on the last one.

"Because I let you," he says with a satisfied smirk.

"Shut up. I still win."

I wipe my mouth and hope I don't look too weird gobbling up the delicious cheese. There aren't a whole lot of people sitting near us, so I'm probably safe.

Our entrees come next and it's Boeuf Bourguignon. Of course. I've never had it, but it sounds good. There's also a salad of various greens and lots of bread. It's so much food that I don't think I'll be able to finish it all.

"This looks really good," I say. "For this once, you did good, Javier. But you better not order snails or something next time. I don't care how much of a delicacy they are. I'm not eating snails." I shudder at the thought.

"No snails. Maybe that should be a rule." I pull out my phone and add it to the list. It's now the fourth rule.

We start eating and keep talking about more rules. I shoot down a lot of Javi's.

"There will be no rules about nudity," I say. He sticks out his bottom lip in a ridiculous pout.

"You ruin everything."

I roll my eyes.

"Whatever. I'm not eating dinner naked." His eyes light up like he's got another idea. I can guess what it is. "I'm not letting you eat dinner off me while I'm naked either." Can you imagine if I had an itch or had to get up and pee? No way.

"I don't know why I put up with you. You kill all my good ideas," Javi says, shaking his head in shame as he stabs another piece of beef. The bourguignon is unbelievable. So freaking good. I'm tempted to ask Javi if he'll make it for me so I can compare. I bet his is better.

"Good is a matter of perspective."

We start talking about other things, including what our menu will be for the next week. Most of the time Javi just surprises us, but lately he's started taking suggestions.

"How about soup? You've never done soup," I say as I butter my third piece of bread. It's like I hadn't eaten for a week before I came here, but the food is so good I can't stop. I'm definitely going to regret this in a few hours when I won't be able to move.

"I could do soup. What kind?"

"I don't know. Chicken noodle?" He makes a face. "What's wrong with chicken noodle soup?"

"Any idiot could make it. I like something that's a challenge."

He certainly did. Javi almost never makes anything simple. Even nachos are a gourmet affair, but that's mostly because of Jett and Shannon who have some weird obsession with bizarre toppings.

"Fine. How about that one that has the fish and stuff in it?" I say. I can't remember the name of it. I really should start learning more French if I'm going to be dining with Javi.

"Bouillabaisse?" God, I don't care what it is. I just want him to say it over and over again.

"Yeah, that."

He considers that for a moment.

"I could do that. What's your sudden soup obsession?"

I shrug.

"I don't know. I thought maybe soup was something I might be able to make without much help. I mean, how hard can it be? You just throw everything in the pot with liquid, right?"

"Not exactly. But sure, I can make that next week. You sure Shannon would be up for that?" Maybe. I'll have to ask her.

I want to order another beer, but Javi is driving so I'd feel like a bitch for having two when he can only have one.

"Get another. I know you want to," he says as I look at my empty glass.

"Really? I hate to rub it in your face." He waves that off and sets his fork down on his empty plate.

"It's my fault for losing the bet. Go ahead." He motions for the waitress and she saunters over.

"She'll have another beer and I think we'd like to see the dessert menu." I hadn't said anything about dessert, but I definitely want it.

My beer comes as Javi and I look over the desserts.

"I've never had tiramisu and I've always wondered what it is. Can I get that?" I ask. Javi chuckles.

"You don't have to ask me."

"But you're the one who wants to order."

"So, just tell me what you want."

"I want the tiramisu," I say, jabbing my finger at the menu.

"Shit, I get it. I get it." I kick him again under the table and this time I connect with his shin.

"Ouch. That wasn't necessary."

"It definitely was." The waitress comes back and Javi orders the tiramisu and the chocolate cake.

"That way we can swap back and forth. It's like getting two desserts." I can't argue with his logic.

"So, what did you think?" I say as we wait for the desserts to come.

"Nice place. Good food. Little too much thyme in the bourguignon, but other than that, it was good." I concur, although I don't know about the thyme thing. It tasted amazing to me.

Our desserts come and I excuse myself to head to the restroom.

"Rule Five: When someone's in the bathroom, the other person doesn't touch their dessert," I say before I stand up. Javi just gives me an innocent look.

"I would never do such a thing."

"Right," I say, touching his shoulder as I walk by. The beers were in tall glasses, so it's like I've had almost four. I make my somewhat-unsteady way to the bathroom. Shouldn't have gotten that second beer.

I come back and sit down and there's a huge bite taken out of my tiramisu.

"You bastard. I trusted you," I say with a glare. I pick up my butter knife and point it at him. "You've betrayed me, Javier Cruz, and I don't take betrayal lightly." He just gives me the innocent look.

"I have no idea what you're talking about," he says, but I wipe the side of his mouth with my finger.

"Yup. That doesn't look like chocolate. How could you?" I keep my voice low, but I can feel people looking at me, like Javi and I are having a real fight. It's kind of hilarious.

Javi plays along with me.

"I'm sorry! I didn't mean to do it. I swear, it will never happen again. This was the only time." I brandish my knife and then grab my fork.

"The only way to solve this is a bite for a bite." I take a giant scoop out of his piece of cake and shove it in my mouth.

"An eye for an eye leaves the whole world without cake," he says and I nearly choke, but manage chew and swallow the massive bite of cake.

I go back to my tiramisu and Javi keeps trying to steal bites, but I just knock his fork away with mine.

"You're not very good at sharing, are you?" he says. "Must be an only child."

"I'm not an only child," I retort, and then realize I didn't mean to tell him that. I don't want to answer questions about my family.

"Oh?" he says, like he's not really that interested, but I know he is. "So, how many siblings do you have?" I grab another bite of his chocolate cake.

"How many do you have, Javier?" Take that. I can answer a personal question with a personal question.

"I asked you first. How about that as another rule? The person who asks first has to be answered first." I shake my head. No, I'm not agreeing to that rule.

"Why don't you want to talk about your family?" Javi says in a low voice.

"Why don't you want to talk about yours? This goes both ways. You can't be mad at me for not talking about my life when you don't talk about yours. How about we make that a rule? If one of us asks a question, they have to also be willing to answer it themselves." Javi narrows his eyes, but nods. I add that to the list as Rule Six.

"Okay then. So, why don't you want to talk about your family?" he asks again.

"And if I tell you, you'll answer when I ask you?" He sighs and then nods again.

"Fine. I don't talk about my family because I don't like my family. I'm not even sure there's love there. Not even that kind of obligatory love you're supposed to have for people you're related to. Neither of my parents gave a shit about me, and my siblings didn't either. They were all too busy drinking and doing drugs and sitting around and yelling at sports games and being general wastes of space. None of them even graduated high school and forget about college. They think I'm crazy for working so hard when I could just go out, get knocked up and live off the system."

I shudder. That's what my sisters and my brother had done. All three of them had kids before they turned 18. My mom practically encouraged it. She worked part time flipping burgers at whatever place would take her and Dad would do odd jobs whenever the lights and water got shut off. His main job was sitting on the couch and drinking beer and yelling at the television.

Yes, I know I shouldn't hate them, but I do. They would bitch and complain and moan about how shitty their lives were, but wouldn't do a damn thing to change them; then they made fun of me for actually trying to make something of myself. It's one of the things that drives me so hard to be a lawyer. I don't want to end up like that. I won't waste my life.

"So there you go. I have two sisters and one brother and I've only talked to them once or twice in the past year. They're much too busy having babies and breaking up and getting married and sometimes getting arrested." I do the one-shoulder shrug. I hate talking about this. It just throws me into a depressive state that can sometimes take days to recover from. It's one of the reasons I got out as soon as I graduated high school. I would have gotten out sooner if I could have made it happen.

"Your turn." I finish my tiramisu (which was outstanding) and sit back and wait for him to tell his story.

"I can understand why you wouldn't want to talk about them. I'm sorry they were so shitty to you. Is it weird that I want to meet them so I can yell at them on your behalf?" I thought we were going to be talking about him, but we're still on me.

"They wouldn't listen to you. They hate anyone who actually does anything with their life, and they hate people who go to college and think they're better than everyone else. I know it makes no sense, but they don't really live by logic." One of the reasons I don't see my parents is that I'm treated to a lecture about how I think I'm too good for them now that I'm a college girl. The phrase "uppity bitch" is often bandied about.

"My family… I don't talk about them because…" Javi can't seem to get the words out. "My family is all in prison."

"What?" That wasn't what I expected. At all. I thought maybe he was one of those people who was from a rich family, but he didn't want anyone else to know so he pretended to be poor.

"My family is all in jail. Well, or they're out on parole. Mom, Dad, all my brothers and sisters-in-law. Even some of my nieces and nephews." Wow, it sounded like he was from a huge family. A huge criminal family.

So I ask the question that anyone else would have asked.

"What are they in prison for?" Javi meets my eyes and holds contact for a few seconds before he answers.

"Drugs. Murder. Fraud. Money laundering. You name it, they've done it." Holy fucking shit.

This restaurant doesn't feel like the right setting for talking about this. Honestly, I'm a bit uncomfortable. The waitress brings the check and interrupts Javi. He pulls out some cash and puts it in the envelope.

"No change, thank you so much." He hands it back to her and then his attention is back on me.

"Are you shocked?"

"Well, that's a silly question. Of course I'm shocked. I didn't think…" I can't finish my sentence.

"I know. And now you know why I didn't tell you. Why I don't tell anyone. There's a reason I came to Maine. No one knows me here. People aren't afraid of me when I walk around. It's nice." Whoa, this is getting more and more intense and I think I need a moment.

"I'm sorry for dropping all this on you. I probably should have taken a more gentle approach." He starts to get up and I do the same. I wobble a little bit on my feet and I don't know if it's the beers or the weight of the information on my shoulders.

"I'm sorry," he says again.

"No, no," I say, finding my voice. The words keep sticking in my throat. "It's a lot. And I shouldn't have asked if I didn't want to know. So really, it's my fault. I want to know more, but I don't know if I want to know right now." He nods and leads me to the door where the hostess wishes us a good night.

I let Javi open the door of the truck and boost me in. I shiver, even though it was warm in the restaurant.

Javi gets in the truck and starts it. The radio blasts on and he turns it off. The GPS on my phone starts yapping, but I turn it off as well.

"I'm not ready to back to the apartment. Just drive somewhere. Anywhere," I say. I don't care. I just need to sit in a moving car and think for a while.

"Sure," Javi says and pulls out of the parking lot.

Chapter Sixteen

We get further and further from civilization and finally Javi pulls into the driveway of what looks like an abandoned house. The paint is peeling and the grass so overgrown it reaches all the way to the windows on the first floor. There's no evidence of human life anywhere.

"Where are we?" I ask as he turns the engine off.

"I have no idea. I figured your phone could get us back. So."

"So." It's so quiet out here. Too quiet.

"I'm sorry if I'm being weird. I just don't know how to react, or what to say, and I don't want to say the wrong thing, so I was trying to think of something to say and I couldn't think of anything." God, I sound like Shannon.

Javi rubs his hands on the steering wheel.

"Yeah, I figured. It's no big deal. I can understand what a shock it must be. Sometimes I can't believe it's my life either, even though I wasn't really around it much." I open my mouth to ask a question, but he cuts me off and keeps talking.

"I was raised by my grandmother. I was the youngest and she figured she could get me out and keep me safe. My parents didn't really care all that much since they had all my brothers to carry on the family legacy, so to speak, so they gave me up to her. But they would come by every now and then. And I couldn't avoid the news, or what people said about me. She… she died a few years ago." His voice shook.

"I'm so sorry, Javi." He just keeps breaking my heart. My childhood sucked, but it wasn't even close to that. Sure, my family dabbled in drugs, but nothing too hard and they weren't dealers.

"She was the only one who ever cared about me as anything other than a cog in a wheel. She's the reason I'm in college. It was her dream for me." I can't stop the tears from coming, but I brush them away so he won't see them.

"There's more, but those are stories for another time." He sighs and I can sense he's done for now. I wipe my eyes and sniff. I really need a tissue.

"In the glove box," Javi says and I pull out a travel pack of tissues and blow my nose.

"I'm sorry. I didn't mean to cry."

"It's okay." His voice is hollow.

"Do you regret telling me?" I ask. He thinks about that for a moment.

"I don't know. The only other person who knows is Jett. He's got his own family drama, so we sort of bonded over that. Not that his parents are criminals, but he understands the need to get away from your genetics."

"I get that. So does Shannon. Her family is also pretty shitty. Man, what are the chances we'd all find each other?" Miniscule. There wasn't one of us who had a "typical" upbringing, whatever that was.

"Pretty good. I think most people, if you really asked them, would tell you they had bad stuff in their lives. That's life. Bad stuff happening and then good stuff happening in between. And sometimes the bad comes with the good." I move close to him. The truck is getting cold and I want to ask him to turn the heat on.

The house in front of us looks sad and abandoned, almost like it's crying.

"So, Javi. Is this bad or good?"

"Both," he says and then reaches for me. I lean into him, the seats in the truck creaking.

He kisses me softly and I wait for it to escalate. But he pulls away and strokes my face.

"You look really amazing tonight. I just wanted you to know that. And I had a really good time on our non-date. I can't wait to do it again."

"Ditto," I say and sit back.

We both stare at the house for a few minutes, and then the shivering becomes too much for me.

"Ready to go back?" I nod and Javi turns the truck back on and I get out my phone to figure out where the hell we are and how to get back to my apartment.

"Are you sure you don't want me to go?" Javi says when he parks the truck.

"Only if you want to. If you want to stay, stay. If you don't, don't." He nods and gets out of the truck and then opens my door.

"You're not supposed to do that," I say.

"Fuck the rules." He takes my hand as we walk up the porch and into the house. It's quiet and Shannon has left a note that she's staying at Jett's. She could have just texted me like she usually does, but I have the feeling she didn't want to interrupt my non-date.

Javi keeps my hand in his and leads me to my bedroom.

He lets go only to pull the cardigan off my shoulders and turn me around.

"Fuck, I love this dress." His fingers trace the straps that crisscross in the back. His lips kiss my bare shoulder and I lean back into him.

"Javi," I say, my voice all breathy. God, what he does to me with just a few touches and a kiss.

"Shhh," he says. "Let me take care of you."

He pulls the straps over my shoulders and kisses across my upper back. I had to wear a strapless bra, so he undoes that and then unzips the dress. It falls to the floor and then he moves us to stand in front of my closet where I have a full-length mirror.

"Look how beautiful you are," he says in my ear as he hooks his fingers around the edges of my panties and then slowly lowers them down my legs. He looks up at me and I almost want to cry again. He's looking at me with so much… love.

There's nothing else it can be. It's one of those things. You know it when you see it. And there it is.

He picks up my foot and kisses my ankle and moves upward to the inside of my leg, lifting and putting it over his shoulder. I shudder and can barely stand and he hasn't even gotten to the good part yet.

"Watch yourself. I want you to see what I see." I've never been much of an exhibitionist, but I look in the mirror. Javi is on his knees, my leg hooked over his shoulder and I'm arching into him. My skin is flushed and my eyes are bright. Excited.

Javi kisses further up my leg and I watch myself and watch him. He keeps glancing up at me to make sure I'm watching myself.

He turns us a little so I can watch as he sticks his tongue out and licks even further upward. Watching him like this is…

Now I know why people film themselves having sex.

He licks me slowly and my leg nearly buckles. I have to reach my hands out and put them on the wall to balance myself.

"Keep watching, Haze."

I do.

I watch as he licks me and then strokes me with his fingers, alternating both until I can barely hold myself up. Fortunately, if I fall, he'll sort of catch me.

He blows on me and I convulse, nearly taking him out. He chuckles and takes my leg off his shoulder.

"We'll have to work on that one, gorgeous," he says as he picks me up and carries me to the bed and lays me down. I can no longer see both of us in the mirror, but the memory of it is still making me burn.

Javi resumes his position between my legs and with lips and tongue and fingers he finishes me off and the climax rockets through me, going on and on and on. Javier knows my body enough to know how to keep it going. He's… incredible. Just incredible.

"Did you like that?" he asks, laying his head on my stomach.

"That was new."

"I thought you might want to see what I see. I know it gets me off." He grins and I run my fingers through his hair.

"For a guy who seems like a pig, you certainly know how to push all the right buttons." I shiver with a little aftershock as Javi kisses right below my navel.

"Pleasuring you gets me off. So it's not as altruistic as it seems."

"Still. I love it."

He grins at me again and I pull his face up so I can kiss him as I reach down to stroke him through his pants. He hasn't even taken his shoes off.

"My turn." I hook my legs around him and flip us over so I'm on top. I laugh as I start unbuttoning his shirt.

"You know, if you want to have sex with me every day, all you have to do is wear this outfit. Because yeah. It's fucking hot."

"Really?" Javi says, putting his hands behind his bed as if he's relaxing. "Well, I shall have to add more dress shirts to my wardrobe. Would a suit earn me two rounds?"

"Three and an extra blow job," say. He raises one eyebrow as I open the shirt to reveal his white tank top underneath. The thing is so thin I can see the black ink of his tattoos bleeding through it, like ink paper.

I move back so he can sit up as I pull the shirt over his head. His shoes are the next victims and then his pants.

I finally have him the way I really want him, although the undressing part was kind of fun.

"You don't have to," he says as I kiss my way over his chest and down south.

"I get off on it too," I say before licking him at the tip. I wish he could see what I see when I go down on him. The control I have when he's in my mouth, or inside me is so erotic, and sometimes I reach my hand between my legs and get myself off at the same time.

"Oh, fuck, Hazel." His fingers twist in my hair and pull a little, but I like it like that. A little bit of pain never hurt anyone.

I go to town on him and this time he comes in my mouth. It's not my favorite thing in the world, but it's tit for tat. Or dick for clit. Something like that.

"Thank you," he pants as I smile up at him.

"You're welcome, Javier."

"Haze?" Javi says when we're both satiated and I'm half-asleep. My body is heavy from the food and the beer and the sex. It's pretty much the best combination ever. Better than Thanksgiving.

"Yeah?" I open my eyes and look up at him.

"Thank you for tonight. For listening."

"You're welcome. And thank you for telling me. I know that can't have been easy." He sighs and kisses my hair.

"It wasn't. But I'm glad it was you I told. I'd rather be here with you right now than anywhere else." I trace the lines of his tattoos with one finger.

"Not even Vegas?" I ask.

"Not even Vegas. That's not really my scene anyway. I prefer New York." I sit up so I can see his eyes through the darkness.

"New York City?"

He nods.

"Yeah. I love New York. I wanted to live there, but I chose Maine because Mimi said she always wanted to live here."

"Mimi?"

"That was what I called my grandmother."

"Tell me about her."

"What do you want to know?"

"What was she like?"

He chuckles and looks away from me, like he's watching a movie of his past that I can't see.

"She cursed like a fucking sailor for one thing. And she didn't trust anyone. And she kept a gun under her bed, just in case. She used to carry one under her knitting when she had to ride the bus."

"She sounds like a total badass."

He laughs again and wipes his eyes, like he's wiping away tears.

"She would love to hear you say that. I know she would have liked you." He tells me more about her, how she didn't put up with shit from anyone, and pinched her pennies so much that she was able to save a small amount to send Javi to college, which he only found out about after she died.

"The money I have? The money for the bed and for my education and all that? It's from my family." Oh. There it is. The question I've had since he started buying us groceries.

"I used to just ignore it, but then I decided that if I had it, I might as well use it for something. Use it for good." That explains a lot.

"Most of it has gone to charities or people who were there for me and helped me out when I was young and Mimi couldn't afford to feed us. Soup kitchens and church charities and so forth. I use some of it for my education and now I'm using some of it on you." He's using crime money on me?

"Javi?"

"Yeah."

"You said your family killed people."

"They do. They have."

"So that money has blood on it."

"Would it be any better if they were part of an oil company that destroyed the environment? Or used child labor? Most money is dirty. And I've learned you don't get a lot of money unless you get pretty dirty." He has a point, but I'm sure there are plenty of people who have money who didn't have to kill anyone to get it, or do something else equally awful.

"That doesn't mean you have to take it." He makes a sound of frustration.

"Look, all the things you're thinking right now? I've thought before. I've spent my whole life being haunted by this money. Being sick at the thought of it. And I finally decided that this money is going to exist, no matter what I do with it. And once I take it away from my family and use it for something good, it takes away a little bit of their power over me. Over my life. It's my subtle way of getting back at them."

I think about that for a little while, listening to the beat of his heart. It's fast.

"I guess. It is your money. Why did they give it to you? They must know what you're doing with it." His fingers start moving up and down my spine in slow circles. It's very soothing, despite the intensity of what we're talking about.

"Would they ever come after you?" I whisper.

He shakes his head.

"No. They've given up on me. And the money was mine when I was born. It's mine to do with what I want. They live by a set of rules that doesn't make sense to most people, but it's ironclad. No matter what I do, the money is mine." That is strange, but he's the one who lives it. He should know. Still, I'm going to look over my shoulder. I guess you never know about people.

"Where are you from?" He hadn't mentioned this during the initial questioning.

"We moved around a lot. I was born in New York, but lived most of my life in Texas." Huh. He didn't have an accent. Someone else would probably say he had one, but to me he didn't.

"Did you like it?"

"There were good times. It was definitely warmer down there, which was nice. I'm not a huge fan of winter." Me neither.

"I've never lived outside of Maine. I've never even been out of the state," I admit. This is one of those things I don't tell a whole lot of people. Only Shannon knows.

"Really? You've never been anywhere else?" I keep tracing his tattoos. They're quite remarkable.

"No. I always wanted to. My plan was to get the hell out of this state, but then the lure of a scholarship made me stay."

"Well, I think we should definitely plan a road trip. I'll take you to New York. I think you'd love it. We'll do Times Square and Central Park and all the standard places, but I'll take you to other places too. There's some beautiful spots if you're willing to search just a little bit." The idea of New York City overwhelms me, but I don't tell Javi that.

"I think I'd be okay with that. Maybe this summer?" I'm breaking my own rule about not talking about the future.

"Sure. We'll do a road trip, just the two of us. Or we could invite Shannon and Jett if you want." I'm not sure, this summer is still a long way off. But I like the idea of having plans with Javi a few months from now.

"Sounds perfect," I say and close my eyes. "You don't have to talk about yourself anymore. Unless you want to." I yawn.

"No, go to sleep. I can be done for tonight. And we have tomorrow to talk. And hopefully the next day, if we play our cards right." I nod and rest my head against his chest.

"Goodnight, Javier."

"Goodnight, Hazel."

Chapter Seventeen

My head spins for the next few days, thinking about Javier's life. To be honest, it sounds like something out of a movie, or a sensational novel. But it isn't. It's real and it's his life.

"Do you know how to use a knife?" I ask while we're making dinner the next night. He looks at me like I'm crazy. "What? I've been thinking of all these weird questions now that I know about your past and all."

"Okay. I'm not going to try and follow the weird logic your brain follows. Um, no, I don't know how to use a knife in the way you're suggesting. I can chop and I guess if I had to defend my life or someone else's, I could hold my own. Maybe. I don't know. I never tried."

He stirs the vegetables in the bottom of the brand new soup pot he brought over.

"But if you'd stayed with your family would you know how to use it for things other than chopping?" He stares into the pot.

"Probably. I'd know a lot of other things. How to shoot, how to fight with my fists, how to pick pockets." I look at him with an objective eye, but I can't see him as anything other than my Javier. The guy who broke my bed, but who makes me dinner every night and was there for my best friend when I wasn't.

He's just my Javier. I can't pinpoint the exact moment when I decided to call him mine, to claim him so no one else could have him, but I can't un-think it.

"We don't have to talk about it," I say softly, putting my arm around his waist. He puts his arm around me and holds me close.

"It's okay. You're curious. It's not a sin in my book." I close my eyes and inhale his scent.

"Are you smelling me?" he asks, ruining the moment.

"No. I was just... Okay. So what? I was smelling you. You smell really good. I can't help it."

"You smell good too, gorgeous." He used to have sort of a snarky tone when he called me that. But now it's... it's a term of endearment.

"Good. I'd hate to smell bad to you."

"Never. Not even if you rolled in garbage."

Gross.

Shannon and Jett walk through the door, which ends the smelly discussion.

Neither of them looks pleased.

"Everything okay?" I say, sharing a look with Javi. He puts his cooking utensils down and goes to the fridge to get both of them a beer. There's also a bottle of whiskey in there that I don't remember buying.

"Yeah," Shannon says, sitting down in her usual chair and putting her head in her hands.

"Fine," Jett agrees, heading to the bathroom. Whoa. I've never seen them quite like this before. Usually when they fight you can tell how much they want to make up and stop being mad at each other.

"What's wrong?" I say, going to Shannon and sitting down next to her.

"We had a fight, that's all. He asked me to move in with him."
Her face is blotchy and starting to get red. It's clear she's been crying.

"I think I'm going to go and be wherever Jett is," Javi says, pulling
the bottle of whiskey out of the fridge and grabbing two glasses from
the dish drainer. Typical Javi.

I reach out and put my arm around Shannon.

"Tell me what happened."

Shit, she looks absolutely miserable.

"It's just what I said. He asked me to move in with him and I was
a bitch and now everything is fucked up." She starts to cry and I grab
a napkin and hand it to her.

"How is it fucked up? Did you say yes?"

"Obviously not. I said no. I mean, shit, we've barely been dating
and I'm already living with you. And I hate his apartment." She wails
the last part and then totally breaks down.

"It's so gross and I'm always afraid I'm going to fall through the
floor and the pipes make weird noises at night and his creepy neighbor
is always staring at me," she says in between sniffing and wiping her
eyes.

"So you could get a new place. Or maybe Jett could move in here."
I don't mean to suggest that, since it's already crowded with just me
and Shannon and since Javi's here too, it would be really tight quarters.

"I don't know. I just… He got mad when I said I didn't want to
move to his place and then I said all the reasons I didn't think it was a
good idea and now he's mad at me." She looks up at me with her red-
rimmed eyes and I just want to hug her, so I do.

"You haven't broken anything beyond fixing, Shan. Jett loves you
and you love him. People fight all the time. That's all this is. A fight.
You'll talk and get everything out in the open and then have some
mind-blowing make-up sex and then it will be fine. Trust my Hazel
senses. Okay?" She nods and wipes her nose.

A bad smell reaches my nose and I realize Javi left the stove on too high and now the vegetables are burning.

"Shit!" I get up and turn the pan off, waving my arms to clear the smell and the smoke that's starting to pour from the open pot. The smoke detector chooses that moment to start going off as Shannon and I flail our arms near it to make it stop.

The guys rush out. Javi still has the whiskey bottle clutched in his fist.

"What happened?" he yells over the awful beeping.

"Your soup burned!" I yell back as the beeping finally stops.

The kitchen is still pretty smoky so Shannon opens the front door. It's chilly outside, but at least some of the smell will be gone.

"Shit, that's my bad. I should have turned the pot off. Good thing I bought extra just in case of an emergency like this." He dumps the burned veggies into the trash, washes out the pot and then starts the soup over.

Jett is staring at Shannon and she's staring back at him, her hand on the doorknob.

"Shan," Jett says. "I'm so sorry. I freaked out. I shouldn't have sprung that on you and I shouldn't have flipped when you didn't immediately agree. I'm so sorry, princess." Shannon sniffs and closes the door. I push her toward Jett and she takes his hand and leads him into her bedroom and shuts the door.

"Good. Hopefully that will get things worked out," I say, trying not to listen to what's going on behind the closed door.

"Oh, I think they'll be fine. Love has a way of working out when it's meant to be." I stare at Javi.

"Wow. That was really romantic." He smiles.

"Yeah?"

"Absolutely."

He shrugs.

"Guess I'm just… inspired lately."

I walk toward him.

"I hope I have something to do with it."

He turns away from the stove and faces me.

"You have everything to do with it.

Shannon and Jett don't emerge from her bedroom until the soup is well under way. Javi is trying out the bouillabaisse and there's a fortune's worth of seafood in the pot. I had no idea how expensive it would be or else I wouldn't have asked him to make it.

When the couple does return, Shannon's eyes are still red, but dry and her hair is disheveled. Jett's mohawk looks like it's had fingers in it and his lips are swollen.

"So," I say, looking them up and down. "Everything okay now?"

They nod in unison.

"Yeah," they both say and then take their chairs at the table.

"What's the verdict?" I ask. "Moving in yes or moving in no?"

They exchange a glance.

"We've decided to shelve the idea for now," Jett says. "One of us was a little too eager and might have jumped the gun. One of us named Jett." He laughs and takes Shannon's hand.

"And one of us named Shannon decided that she should probably think before she freaks out about things and starts letting her mouth run." I'll believe that when I see it. Shannon hasn't had a filter as long as I've known her. It's one of her adorable quirks.

"Good. I'm glad things worked out," I say and Javi agrees.

"The whiskey helped too," Jett adds. "I'm pretty fucking buzzed right now."

"Why do you always think shots are the way to fix things, Javi?" Shannon says.

He wipes his hands on a dishtowel and takes his attention away from the steaming pot.

"Because alcohol has a way of making things clearer sometimes." And sometimes it made you do things you would never do sober.

Javi gets some shot glasses down from the cabinet and pours shots for me, himself and Shannon.

"Bottoms up," he says, clinking his glass to mine before downing it in one swallow. I down mine as well while Shannon sips at hers.

"That was fucking hot," Javi says, licking his lips.

"I'm good at swallowing," I say.

"I know." Shannon makes a gagging noise and Jett's face is priceless. I lean over and give Javi a kiss. His lips still burn with the taste of the alcohol.

"We should probably stop making Jett and Shannon uncomfortable," I say.

"Probably."

"Please," Shannon says.

"Yes, please," Jett agrees.

The bouillabaisse is phenomenal and we each have two full bowls. There's also enough left over we can have it for dinner the next night. Javi looks sad at the prospect of leftovers.

"But it means you won't have to cook. Aren't you tired of cooking?" I say.

"No."

"Why don't you open your own restaurant? You'd be so good at it."

He makes a face.

"No. Cooking is a hobby. I'd never want it to be a job. Then I'd probably hate doing it, you know?" I guess. But it seems silly to waste a talent that could make you money. Then again, I don't have a secret cache of money, so maybe it's different for him.

"Sure. It was just an idea. I want you to do whatever you want to do." I smile and he kisses the center of my forehead.

"And that's why you're so awesome. You're more than just a fantastic ass and a great pair of tits. Much more."

"If I agree to give you money, will you stop?" Shannon says. Oh, like I haven't had to listen to her and Jett loudly getting it on in the next room? This is payback.

I look at Javi and we both glance at Shannon at the same time.

"No," we say in unison.

Chapter Eighteen

Javi comes with me to the bar that Saturday night. I don't ask him to, he just offers to give me a ride and then hangs out, drinking glasses of water slowly.

"I could bring you one of those shitty non-alcoholic beers, but really, what's the point?" I say as I pass him on my way to the other end of the bar. He just makes a face at me and salutes me with his water glass.

People are unusually nice and I don't know if it has anything to do with Javier, but I'll take it. I watch as he gets hit on a few times; he smiles at the ladies, but brushes them off. I'm weirdly not jealous. Now, if he flirted back, or gave out his number, I'd be upset, but he doesn't seem to be interested.

I've never seen Javier not interested in the opposite sex. It's a bit strange, honestly.

"She was cute," I say when I have a few moments to catch my breath and have a sip of water.

"Was she?" he says. "I didn't notice." I laugh.

"You're such a liar, but it's okay. I'm not jealous. Besides. I'm not your girl. If you wanted to flirt with her, you could have. I'm not stopping you." I'm interested to see how he'll answer.

"I don't want to flirt with her. She was boring." I didn't talk to her, so I don't know if she's boring or not, but that hadn't stopped him before.

"And? Boring is suddenly a problem for you?" I've seen him flirt with girls who could barely tie their own shoes.

He does the one-shoulder shrug.

"I don't know. Just not in the mood for boring tonight." I get busy again and don't get to even glance at him for an hour.

He's reading.

Javier is sitting at my bar, reading. Like a character from some romance novel. Be still my heart.

"Homework?" I say as the bar starts to empty out and Joe rings the bell for last call.

"No. Just reading."

"For the hell of it?" He looks up and blinks at me. The only thing that would make him hotter right now is a sexy pair of glasses. Maybe I can get a pair without lenses in them.

"Yeah. Why are you looking at me like that?" Crap, I've been caught staring again.

"I'm looking at you because I'm talking to you, Javi. Why do you keep trying to make me looking at you into more than it is?" I'm grateful for the darkness of the bar so he can't see my blush.

"Sure, okay." He goes back to his book and I start doing my side work so I can leave as quickly as possible. Once I'm done, I grab my jacket and hop over the bar.

"Ready?" Javi says, looking up from his book and using a coaster to mark his place.

"Yeah. How was your book? It's a miracle you can even read in this light." Dim lighting seems to be the trend in drinking establishments and this bar is dimmer than others.

"Why are you so obsessed with me reading?" He holds the door for me as we walk toward his truck. A guy waiting for a cab whistles at

139

me and gives me a proposition, but I ignore him. I'd been shocked when I first started bartending, but now it all goes in one ear and out the other. Usually the guys who yell that stuff aren't very creative.

"I've just never seen you reading all that much, except for school. Why is it weird for me to be curious about you?" I hop up in the truck and he swings himself in and lays the book on the seat between us.

I can read the title by the orange glow of the streetlight.

1984 by George Orwell. I think I've seen it on Shannon's shelf, but maybe not.

"So, what's it about?" I ask and he rolls his eyes and turns on the truck.

"It's about the future. Or what could be the future. It's complicated."

"Are there robots?" There are probably robots.

"No. It's about people. It's really good. You can have it when I'm done. I got it from the library, but I can renew it."

"Maybe. I don't read much fiction. I get burned out on reading for school and the last thing I want to do is more reading. My brain can only take so much." Still, I pick up the book and read the back. Huh. Definitely not what I thought it would be.

"I get that. But sometimes reading fiction is more than just reading. You fall into a world that isn't like your own and live in it for a while. Don't you ever want to do that?" He gives me this look and I don't even know what the hell to say.

"That was fucking deep, Javi. What the hell?"

It's really dark, but I swear I can see him blushing.

"Yeah. Well." He stares out the windshield really hard.

"I like it. I like everything about you," I say, sliding closer to him.

"The feeling is mutual, Haze." I give him a kiss on the cheek.

Jett and Shannon have gone to his place, so Javi and I are by ourselves. We take our usual shower together, but he doesn't drag me back to my room to ravish me.

Instead he lays me down in my bed and peels the towel off and just looks at me.

"What are you doing?"

"Just appreciating." Something about the way he's looking at me makes me want to cover myself with my hands. My body is by no means perfect and I'm as sensitive about my flaws as the next girl. But Javi never seems to see the flaws. He just sees me.

He pulls me into a sitting position and wraps me back up in my towel, then gets my brush from the dresser and starts combing out my hair.

"You're very quiet tonight," I say as he untangles my hair with surprising gentleness.

"Just thinking."

"What about?" I look over my shoulder at him. His lips are pursed.

"I don't want to tell you."

"Why not?"

His eyes flick to mine and then skip away.

"Because I'm thinking that I want you to live with me. All the time." I freeze. "I talked with Jett about it and I feel the same way about it as he does. I'm not asking you to live with me, and I'm not saying that we should. I just was thinking about it. How nice it would be."

Words have utterly failed me. I have absolutely nothing to say.

Javi goes back to brushing my hair as I try to get my shit together.

"Does this mean you want me to be your girlfriend?" The brush pauses.

"I guess you could say that. I just… want you."

"The feeling is mutual."

"And I love being around you. I love sleeping with you, and by sleeping I don't mean sex. I love waking up in the middle of the night with you in my arms. I love cooking for you and making you mad and hanging out with you at work." I love all of those things too.

"So what I'm basically saying," he says, kissing my still-damp shoulder, "is that I love you."

Wow. I never thought he'd say those words.

"You do?" I need him to say it again.

"Yeah, I do. Have for a while, but I was scared to say it. I've never said it to anyone but Mimi and maybe Jett when I'm drunk."

I open my mouth and…

"I love you, too."

His smile lights up the room and I've never seen him so happy before. Not even when he's driving me crazy.

"You do? Even though I'm a pain in your ass?" he says.

"Uh huh. And I kind of love that too. No one drives me crazy like you do. And no one has ever made me feel like you do." The sex is amazing, and I know why now. It's because it's not just sex. It's two people who care for each other showing how much they do. I'm so glad we didn't have sex right away when we first met. Because maybe we wouldn't be here now. I'm not taking that as some sort of lesson on waiting to have sex, but things worked out the way I think they were supposed to.

"What do we do now?" I ask. I've never been in this position before. Not so serious. Not so real.

"Well, I think sex is in order. Lots and lots of sex. Or do we call it making love now? I really hate people who call it that." I lean forward and kiss him, pulling away my towel again.

"Me too," I say.

Tonight it isn't just sex. It's not making love, whatever that is. It's... Javier and me. Being together. It's special and beautiful and raw and I don't want it to end.

"I fucking love you," he gasps as he thrusts into me.

"I fucking love you," I say as I hold onto him and ride out the storm.

We go so long and so hard that I'm already considering skipping class the next day. I mention this idea to Javier during one of our breaks.

"You? Play hooky? Never." It's true. Even if I was on my deathbed, I would still make it to class. I'm spending a shit ton on my education, so I might as well get my money's worth. And when I head to law school those days of class could be vital.

"Just this once. For you. Because I love you," I say. I can't shut up about it.

"I love you too." I make a face.

"What?" he says, combing his fingers through my still-drying, sexed-up hair.

"We're those people now. The disgusting, in-love people. I never wanted to be one of those people. I make fun of those people."

"Yeah, well, I never planned on this either. But it's happening and I don't give a shit what anyone else thinks." My stomach flutters at his words.

"As long as you don't call me 'babe' every five seconds. I won't stand for that." If there's one thing that drives me fucking nuts, it's that. Talk about patronizing.

"Hey, babe, do you think you can get me a beer, babe?" he says, pointing at the door.

"You are pushing your luck, babe," I say, narrowing my eyes.

He just laughs.

"Yeah, I don't think that's for us."

"Definitely not," I agree.

His fingers skim over my belly and I can feel the heat building between us again. I honestly don't think I can take another orgasm. It might kill me.

"So what do you want to do with your day off?" he asks.

I shrug one shoulder.

"I don't know. I haven't had a chance to think about it yet." I don't get a whole lot of days off, so I'm not sure what to do with it.

"I'm guessing I can't talk you into going back to the furniture store and getting some pieces to match your bed, can I?" I smack him in the chest. We've been over this already.

"No. You're not buying me any more furniture."

"But what if we move in together? Then can I buy you furniture?"

He's skating on thin ice.

"We'll cross that bridge when we get there. We haven't even been dating yet. We might decide we hate each other."

He gives me a look.

"Oh, I'm sure there will be times that you hate me. And vice-versa. That's how love works. You have to take the hate with the love," he says.

He has a good point.

"So, how about the furniture?" This time I kiss him, thrusting my tongue in his mouth.

"Shut up about the furniture," I say, running my hand down his chest and grabbing his dick. It starts to get hard in my hand.

"Whatever you say, babe."

Chapter Nineteen

We only sleep for a few hours before Shannon bangs through the front door.

"Haze? Javi? Are you here?" she calls.

I open my eyes and groan. My body is sore and sluggish from all the sex.

"Tell me again why you don't want us to get our own place?" he says.

"We're playing hooky!" I yell through the door so I don't have to actually get up and put clothes on.

"You are?" Shannon yells back.

"Yes!"

"Why?"

"Because we're going to have sex all day!" Javi roars.

Shannon is silent for a moment.

"Okay, okay. I get it. Have fun!" The door slams again and the apartment is silent.

"Is that what we're doing all day? Because I don't think I have the strength, babe," I say.

Javi smiles at me.

"Don't worry, babe. I've got other plans."

"Where the hell are we?" I ask a few hours later. After finally getting out of bed, Javi messed around in the kitchen and then brought me a tray of French toast, fruit and coffee. I've never had anyone make me breakfast in bed before.

Now we're in his truck and I have no idea where we're going.

"Do you trust me, babe?"

"Not right now I don't." We're in the middle of nowhere, I swear. All I can see are trees. This is not an uncommon sight in Maine, but it's freaking me out a little. "Right now I'm worried you're taking me to a secluded cabin to murder me, babe."

Javi roars with laughter. It wasn't that funny.

"You'll see where we're going when we get there."

I cross my arms and change the radio station. Javi groans.

"If you're not going to tell me where we're going, then I get to listen to what I want on the radio," I say as Seal's "Kiss From a Rose" plays. I've never actually understood the meaning of this song, but Seal is sexy, so it doesn't really matter.

"Sure, babe," he says and takes another turn.

We drive for what feels like hours, but is probably only one. Javi's truck doesn't have a clock so I can't be sure. The roads are winding and keep getting more and more rural. The trees are so thick that not a lot of sun gets through and it's quite dark.

Javi says something to himself and then makes another turn, slowing down. On the left is a darling little church. It came out of nowhere and looks so out of place with the wildness surrounding it.

Despite being so rural, the church has fresh white paint on it and the bell in the tower is shiny and bright.

"Here we are," Javi says, parking the truck on the grass in front of the church and turning the engine off.

"Where is 'here'?" I'd tried to keep track of the road signs, but I I honestly have no idea where we actually are.

"We're in Rose Hill, and this is the Rose Church." That still doesn't explain anything.

"You're going to have to give me some more information, babe."

"Come with me," he says and gets out of the truck. I do and he takes my hand, leading me toward the church.

"My grandmother wasn't a very religious woman, but she loved churches. She had pictures and books of them all over the house. When I was a kid she would show them to me. This one was her favorite. I don't know why. But before she died, she told me that if anything ever happened to her, she wanted her ashes sprinkled next to this church. So I did." His hand tightens on mine.

He's knocked me speechless twice in less than 24 hours.

"That's beautiful, Javi." My voice breaks. He looks away from the church and smiles at me.

"Thanks. Sometimes I drive here and just… sit. I don't know if I believe in heaven or hell, but I know I believe that if Mimi is anywhere, she'd be here."

We walk all the way around the church. There are flowerbeds in the back, with little green buds just starting to poke through the ground.

"The town has a fund and they have volunteers that come up here and maintain the church. I may have given them a donation or two." I bet he did more than that.

There's also a little flat clearing behind the garden where the sun pours down. The whole thing looks like a postcard.

"Thank you for bringing me here," I say as we stand in the sunshine. Javi turns his face up and closes his eyes. He's so beautiful in that moment it makes me want to cry.

"I love you so much," I say, my voice only a whisper. I don't want to talk too loudly. This is a sacred place and not just because of the church.

I've never been much for religion either, but I love what Javi did for his grandmother. If I believe in anything, I believe in that. And love. I believe in that now, too. I haven't always.

Javi opens his eyes and looks at me.

"I love you. And she would have loved you. I feel like this is a way you could sort of meet her. She was the most important person in my life before you, and I wish, more than anything, that I could create a way for you two to talk." He sits on the ground and I sit next to him.

A butterfly comes out of nowhere and starts flapping around us.

"Isn't it too cold for butterflies to be out?" I say as it dances around us and then lands on Javi's head.

"I have no idea," he says softly, trying not to move. If I hadn't left my phone in the car I would take a picture of him with the butterfly on his head. It sits on Javi for a little while and then flutters around us and lands on my shoulder.

"Hello," I say, looking down at it as it slowly flaps its wings while it sits on me.

And then it's gone as quick as it came and Javi and I are alone in the sun.

"It's so pretty here. I wonder what it was like when people actually came to this church," I say, looking back at it.

"There was a little village nearby, but it's pretty much gone now. There are a lot of places like that around. There was a mill that supported most of the people here, but it closed so people moved on."

"Sad."

"Yeah, it is." Javi lies back and I lie next to him. He puts his arm around me and I have to close my eyes because the sun is so bright.

I'm drowsy and the sun isn't helping. I snuggle into Javi and let myself relax. We both sigh.

"She would have loved you," Javi whispers and that's the last thing I hear before I fall asleep.

The next thing I know, the sun has moved in the sky and I'm stiff from lying on the grass. I look over and Javi is still asleep, but the second I move, his eyes open.

"Hi."

"Hey," he says, pulling me on top of him. Oh. Is this happening now?

He runs his hands up and down my back and I can tell what his intentions are.

"I can't. Not here. Not after you told me your grandmother is watching you here." I look up, like she's going to be standing right there and glaring at us.

Javi chuckles.

"That's okay, babe."

I get off him and he sits up.

"Are you hungry? I brought some food." We go back to the truck and he pulls the tailgate down before lifting me up and setting me on it and hopping up beside me. From the cooler in the back he pulls a few sandwiches, some chips and some sodas. He must have packed us some food while I was in the shower this morning.

Of course, the sandwiches are not your run-of-the-mill PB&J. They're prosciutto and Havarti with spinach and dill mayo.

We munch on our sandwiches and stare out at the trees.

"Since we did something so... intense this morning, I figured we could do something less intense later. Got any ideas?" he says. I think for a moment.

"Sure. I've got an idea. But you're going to have to let me drive when we get back to the highway." He grunts. Yeah, I figured he wouldn't like me driving his truck. Even though it's nothing special, guys are weird like that about their vehicles.

"I guess."

"I'm not going to wreck your truck, babe." He shrugs one shoulder.

"I guess."

I roll my eyes and steal his bag of chips since mine is empty.

"You're lucky I love you, babe." I chomp loudly on the chips and grin at him.

Javi gets us back to the highway and pulls off at a rest stop so we can switch.

"Just be careful. Don't burn out my clutch." I motion for him to move so I can get in the driver's seat. He finally does.

"Don't worry, babe. I'll buy you a new one." It was only fair.

He winces as I shift out of Park and put the truck in gear. My car is a standard, so I know how to drive stick, but his truck is a bit different from my little sedan.

"Wow, I feel powerful up here." I look down from my new height. This is pretty sweet.

"I could get used to this," I say and head toward the exit so I can get back on the highway.

Every time I shift, Javi winces next to me. It's both irritating and hilarious.

"You're acting like I'm physically hurting you. Calm down." I reach over and pat his shoulder.

"This truck and I have been through a lot together. It's hard to explain," he says. I really am taking as much care as I can so I don't know what more he wants from me. Maybe this was a bad idea.

"If it bothers you so much, you pick the radio station." That seems to cheer him up a little and he goes straight for the classic rock. I have no idea what the song is, but Javi starts singing along and banging out a beat on the dashboard.

I head south and find the exit I'm looking for. I haven't been here for a few years, but I remember the way. I used to come here in high school all the time.

"How good are you at climbing fences?" I ask, a few minutes before we get there.

"Fences?"

"Yeah, chain-link specifically."

"I've done it a few times." I can imagine.

"Good."

"Where the hell are we going?" he asks, almost whining.

"This is just karma, babe. You did the same thing to me this morning."

I finally pull into the old abandoned lot. I've come here plenty of times and never been caught so I'm not worried.

"What's this?" Javi asks, squinting out the dashboard.

"Every teenager's dream. Abandoned amusement park. It shut down in the 90s and no one's taken responsibility for it." I get out of the truck and toss the keys to Javi. He catches them and shoves them back in his pocket.

There are a ton of faded flyers on the fence, but I've never paid attention to them before.

I look around for the wooden crate I used to use to boost myself up and find it piled near some cinderblocks. Guess someone else has been coming here too.

Javi gets up first and climbs the fence like a pro, sitting on the top and reaching down for me. I hook my feet in the links and he hoists me up and then we both turn and drop to the ground.

"Good job, babe," I say, panting a little. Guess I was in better shape in high school, although I didn't work out then either.

We both gaze out at the abandoned park with its broken-down Ferris wheel, busted carousel and empty snack stands.

Everything is peeling paint and faded colors. It makes me sad, but in a good way.

"Spooky," Javi says as we walk toward the Ferris wheel.

"It is. But I like it anyway." Javi doesn't ask if it's safe to wander around here. I like that.

"I used to come here in high school when I wanted to get away from my family. People used to have parties and shit here, but I'd come when no one was around."

He steps over a tipped over trashcan and I kick at a rusted can.

"Come on," I say, leading him to my favorite spot.

There's a machine with swings hanging from it that used to whip them around, but it's long since stopped working. I climb the rickety platform and Javi follows. The swings hold two people, so I get in one and Javi gets in next to me.

"Don't worry, they're secure. And we wouldn't go very far." The swings only hang a few feet off the ground.

Javi puts his arm around me and we rock, banging our swing into the one next to it.

"I almost feel like we're the last two people on earth, you know?" he says quietly.

"Yeah. When I wanted to feel alone, this is where I'd come. I liked feeling alone. I don't anymore though." I've been a loner much of my life, but it never really worked. I like being around people. Shannon, Jett and Javi and my other friends.

"That makes me sad, but I know what you mean. But now you don't have to be alone anymore," he says and I turn and look at him.

"That's good. Being alone sucked."

"Yeah, babe, it did."

We don't stay long at the park, but Javi and I find one of the booths with the stupid games. It's the one where you toss the balls at the milk bottles and try to knock them down. A lot of the bottles are broken or missing, but we find a few and set them up.

"I'm not going to play you because you're definitely going to win," I say. I don't need to see him throw the ball to know he'd kick my ass at this particular game.

"Aw, come on, babe. Please? Not even if I let you win?" He can be very persuasive when he wants to be.

"If you do it with your eyes closed."

He raises one eyebrow.

"Fine." He turns toward the setup of bottles and closes his eyes before he pulls his arm back and throws the ball.

It slams right into the middle of the bottles and knocks every single one down.

I make a disgusted sound and he opens his eyes.

"I didn't mean to make that happen."

"Sure, babe. Whatever." He goes to set up the bottles again and hands me one of the balls.

"Your turn."

I do my best and knock down all but three of the bottles.

"Not bad. You've got a good arm. Your form just needs work." Javi comes behind me and brings my arm back and positions my body.

"You're doing that thing," I say, leaning back into him. I can't help it.

"What thing?" he says in my ear.

"That thing where guys pretend to show a girl how to do something, but it's just so they can feel them up and not be a total creep about it, while actually being a creep about it." He laughs and the movement vibrates against my back and reminds me of all the things we did last night.

It's safe to say that Javi and I are adventurous when it comes to sex. Short of adding another person to the mix (which I'm definitely not up for), neither one of us has a lot of reservations.

"I'm not being creepy, am I?" he says, pushing his pelvis into my back. We were in this very position last night, only we were horizontal.

"No, you're making me want to take your pants off."

"Good." He grinds against me again.

"You're being bad, babe."

"You love it, babe."

I do. I absolutely love it.

So I whip around and kiss him hard before grabbing his hand and dragging him against the wall of the booth.

"You ever had sex in an abandoned amusement park before?" I ask as I push his shirt up.

"Nope. But I'm definitely willing to try." He pulls out a condom from his back pocket. Always prepared, my Javier.

"Good." Getting completely naked isn't practical, so we just pull things down and push them up and before I know it, Javi is pushing me against the wall and fucking me standing up. I wrap one leg around him and he holds onto it and uses it as leverage to go deeper.

I am a little sore, but I seriously don't care, especially when Javi reaches a hand between us and rubs just above our point of connection, driving me even further toward the peak of pleasure.

We both come fast. Afterward, he rests his head on my shoulder and lets my leg down.

"Did you plan that?" I grin at him.

"Nope. Inspiration struck so I thought I should go with it." His smile matches mine.

"You should always go with your inspiration, babe. Always."

After the sex we wander back to the truck. Javi shakes the lock on the fence, but it's not going anywhere. I really don't feel like climbing back over, but we don't have a choice. The sun is going down and the likelihood of someone else showing up and seeing is growing higher. I'm sure many a drug deal has been conducted on these premises.

"I have some tools in the truck I might be able to break this with, but that probably wouldn't be a good idea."

"Probably not," I say as he starts pulling himself up the chain-link fence. I'm all wobbly as I slowly try to climb. Yeah, I had definitely been in better shape in high school. Maybe I should start working out or something.

I finally get to the top of the fence.

"That sucked," I say as Javi hops down.

"Then let me catch you," he says, holding his arms open.

I'm dubious about the drop, but I throw myself down and he does catch me, my feet clattering against the ground a little.

"I got you, babe." I start humming the song by Sonny and Cher as we walk back to the truck.

"You think you can get back to the highway?" I ask as I reach for the passenger door.

"Yes." He gives me a look that makes me not argue with him. Note to self, Javi is protective of his truck.

"You hungry?" I say as we bounce down the road and away from the park. "There's a pizza place not that far from here." I give him directions as he drives.

"Is it even open?" Javi asks when we arrive, and I point to the barely-on neon sign that sputters and almost goes out before it flares to life again.

The place is nothing more than a glorified trailer that someone made into a pizza place by adding some tables and making the kitchen bigger.

A bell tinkles as we walk in and a few people look up at us.

"What do you want, babe?" I ask Javi as he reads the menu written in marker on a whiteboard and hung on the wall.

"I'm good with whatever you want, babe." He pulls me close and gives me a kiss on the cheek. The bored guy behind the counter just waits for us to be done.

"Pepperoni. And pineapple," I say. Maybe we can do with pizza what Jett and Shannon did with nachos.

"That actually sounds good, babe." Javi says and grabs my ass. I give him a look to tell him to cool it. I'm all fine and dandy if he wants to get grabby with me when we're alone, but I draw the line at public groping. And that time he went down on me in the mirror doesn't count.

We order a large pepperoni and pineapple and get sodas out of a machine that sounds like it's on its last legs. The table we pick is covered in one of those red and white plastic checkerboard tablecloths like you'd have at a barbecue.

"This is, uh, a nice place," Javi says, looking around. There's a water stain on the ceiling that kind of looks like Abraham Lincoln. I point it out to Javi.

"Oh yeah, it kind of does. With that little piece at the top for his hat."

We sip our watered-down and practically flat sodas as the people in the kitchen have some sort of dispute. If I remember correctly, the entire place is run by one family. Mother, father, their kids and a few uncles and nieces and nephews.

"That doesn't sound good," Javi says as there's a clatter in the back, followed by more yelling.

"Yeah, I have no idea how this pizza is gonna turn out. It might be awful."

It probably will be.

But being here with Javi, at this crappy pizza place, I'm so fucking happy, I want to jump on the table and burst into song like someone from a musical.

"What's with the face?" Javi asks as the door tinkles and two more people come in. They're both sullen and look like they'd rather be anywhere else. In fact, most of the people in here have that look.

"What face?" I wasn't aware of making any particular face.

"You look so happy." He seems surprised.

"I am," I say and lean across the table to give him a kiss as the guy who took our order announces that our pizza is ready.

"Good. I like seeing you happy. I like to think I have some part of it."

"A big part," I say as he goes to get the pizza and I get some plates, napkins and silverware.

The pizza is massive and actually doesn't look that bad. They loaded us up with the pepperoni and pineapple.

"I take back what I said earlier about this pizza sucking. It kind of looks amazing," Javi says. Probably why this place is still in business. It sure doesn't have anything to do with the fabulous atmosphere and impeccable décor.

"Well, we haven't eaten it yet, so don't get ahead of yourself," I say as we each take a steaming piece. I decide to wait for a moment to give mine a chance to cool, but Javi just bites in and then winces.

"You shouldn't have done that," I say. He sucks air into his mouth and sets the piece down.

"Fanks, I fink I burned my fung." I don't need a translator for that one.

"Serves you right. Didn't your mother ever teach you not to mess around with things that are hot?" Too late I realize my mistake.

Javi gives me a grim smile.

"Sorry, I wasn't thinking. I shouldn't have said that," I say. He shrugs one shoulder and wipes his mouth with a napkin.

"It's okay. It's not your fault. And yes, Mimi did teach me how to avoid hot things. She didn't pull any punches. She told me not to touch the stove, since it was hot. Of course I had to test that and I burned my entire hand. Before she took me to the emergency room, she yelled at me. I was in so much pain that it's a wonder I even remember anything, but it's so clear in my head. I'll never forget how red her face got and how many times she cursed." He grins and I can't even imagine. My parents never really cared about me enough to yell at me. They pretty much ignored me.

I used to do things to try to get them to notice me, but figured out real quick that no matter what I did, short of cutting off my own arm, they weren't going to see me. I was eight when I gave up on them.

I take a bite of the now-cooler pizza and it's really good.

"Wow," I say, my mouth full. Javi takes another bite and agrees.

"You done?" Javi asks when we've eaten all but three slices. Javi really knows how to put it away, but I'm not surprised. I've seen him eat plenty of times.

"Yeah. I don't think I can move. Carry me to the car, babe?"

"If you carry me to the car, babe."

"That's not possible, babe. We can't carry each other."

"Sure we can." I get up and lean on him and tell him to put his arm around me. Like a pair of weirdoes we sort of limp out of the restaurant. Javi's nice and boosts me up into the truck.

"Is it just me, or is your truck cab higher now?" I say once I'm in.

"It's just you, babe." He hauls himself in and we just sit there for a minute.

"Do you want to go back?"

"Sure, I guess. Not much else to do. And I should probably get working on the crap I missed today." Even though I feel a pang of guilt for missing class, I'm glad Javi and I had this day together. We covered a lot of emotional ground in just a few hours together.

"Yeah, I know what you mean. But I wouldn't take this day back. Would you?" he asks as he drives back onto the road.

"Hell no. Today was a little bit perfect, babe."

Javi reaches for my hand and holds it while he shifts. "Indeed it was, babe."

Chapter Twenty

"The delinquents have returned," Shannon says when Javi and I walk through the door, me carrying a box with the leftover pizza.

"Shut up, like you two don't skip class and do stuff," I say, making a face at her and putting the pizza box in the fridge.

"That was different," Shannon says and Jett nods his head. Those two are getting so close sometimes I worry they'll meld into one person.

"How?"

"Because. It was." She lifts her chin in defiance, but I know she's joking.

"Whatever."

"So, how was your day of delinquency?" Jett asks Javi. "I hope you at least did one illegal thing." Javi grins at me.

"We did. Broke into an abandoned amusement park." I hope he doesn't mention the sex that also happened in said amusement park. I'd like to keep that between us. Or at least between me and Shannon. Not that I've ever been closemouthed about my sex life before, but being with Javi is different. Everything is different about this.

"And then my *girlfriend* and I went out and had pizza," he says, putting deliberate emphasis on the word "girlfriend". We didn't talk about how we were going to tell people, but I guess now is as good a time as any.

"Yes, my *boyfriend* let me pick the toppings. That was so nice of you, babe," I say as Shannon gapes at us and Jett looks back and forth from me to Javi.

I just lean into Javi and he puts his arm around me.

"Does this mean you're together, together? Like with definitions and commitment and all that crap?" Shannon says. We both nod and she jumps out of her chair to hug me and then she hugs Javi.

"I thought you two idiots would never come to your senses! It's a miracle!" Jett just gives us a slow clap and Javi glares at him.

"You're hilarious, dude. Fucking hilarious."

I just hug Shannon back.

"Are you crying?"

"No," she says, wiping at her eyes. "I am not crying. Someone must be cutting onions somewhere." She sniffs and starts laughing. I can't help it. I join her and we start jumping up and down and giggling.

"What are they doing?" Javi says, moving away from me.

"I have no idea. But I think we should just let it happen." Jett and Javi slowly back away. Shannon and I just ignore them.

After Shannon and I recover, we all decide that celebratory drinks are in order, so we find some champagne (really, really cheap champagne) in the back of one of our cabinets and bust it out.

Javi makes a face as I pour a glass for him.

"What's with that face?" I ask. He holds the glass up to the light and stares at it, as if it has somehow personally offended him.

"I hate champagne."

"Well, too bad. We're drinking it. I think you'll live," I say as Shannon and Jett raise their glasses.

"To the fantastic foursome," Shannon says and then cringes. "I did not mean that to sound so dirty, like we're in some sort of weird polyamorous relationship. Not that there's anything wrong with polyamory, if that's what you're into. I'm sure it works for some people—" She cuts herself off when Jett squeezes her arm. She's getting better at stopping her rambles before they go off into the distance.

"How about we just clink our glasses so I can drink this stuff and get it over with?" Javi says and I jab him in the ribs with my elbow.

"You're ruining the moment, Javi," I say.

"Let's just toast to, um, boyfriends and girlfriends," Jett suggests and that works for me. We clink our glasses carefully together and sip at the champagne. It's pretty sour, but drinkable. Javi makes a choking sound after his first swallow.

"That is vile stuff. I have no idea how you can drink that."

"Stop being a pussy," I say and force the glass to his lips again. He takes another sip and cringes as he swallows.

"I will drink this entire glass if you promise I never have to drink something like this again," he says.

"Deal," I say, clinking my glass with his again. He tips his up and downs the thing. He shakes his head and then goes to the sink and fills his glass with water and downs that.

"Shit, that's awful stuff."

You'd think I'd just made him drink battery acid.

Jett and Shannon just sip and watch the show.

"Well, next time I'll let you toast with beer, how's that?" I say.

"Whiskey. I want to toast to you with shots of whiskey," he says, coming over and pulling me close.

"Deal," I say and he kisses my lips this time to seal the promise.

"Awww," Shannon says and we break the kiss to glare at her in unison.

The four of us head to the living room to watch a movie after Javi brushes his teeth to get the rest of the champagne taste out of his mouth. Shannon leans on Jett and I lean on Javi and wonder how the hell this actually worked out. What are the chances she'd fall for Jett and I'd fall for Javi? Things just don't work out like that in real life.

I hope it will last. It's perfect right now, but what happens if something goes wrong? And something is very likely to go wrong. That's just the way life works. I know I shouldn't think worst-case-scenario, but it's part of who I am. Always thinking of contingencies. It's my pre-law brain.

"You're thinking about something pretty hard over there," Javi says, pinching the area right above my eyes that wrinkles sometimes when I'm thinking about something.

"Just... thinking about this, that and the other. Nothing special." I'm not going to talk about my thoughts with Javi. Besides, they're probably silly anyway. Who goes into a relationship looking at what's going to happen if it fails?

"Okay," he says, and resumes stroking my hair, but he's probably going to ask me about it later. I know his voice enough to recognize that tone.

Shannon falls asleep again and Jett carries her to bed.

Javi turns the movie off and turns to me.

"Are you worried? About us? Being together and everything." I have to think carefully about my answer.

"Would it bother you if I said yes?"

He shakes his head.

"No. Because I'm worried too. I'm still pretty sure I'm going to screw things up."

"It just seems too perfect. You falling for me and Jett falling for Shannon. The four of us. Two sets of best friends. I mean, it sounds like a cute plot for a romantic comedy with a happily ever after."

"I'm definitely not a happily ever after guy."

"And I'm definitely not that girl." Neither of us belongs in this story. We've been miscast. But here we are anyway.

"I know we shouldn't talk like this," he says. "You know, starting out a relationship thinking of all the ways it's going to go wrong." I'd thought nearly the exact same thing.

"I know. But I guess the only thing we can do is try. If we don't, we'll never know if it could have worked. And despite the potential unpleasantness, I'm really, really glad we're doing this. I just… I love you."

He smiles and pulls my chin toward him and gives me a kiss.

"I love you. Let's not complicate things any more than that." He's right. Right now we're together and that's what matters.

"Ready for bed?" he asks and I nod.

He gets up and leans down.

"Put your arms around my neck." I do and he carries me to bed and gently sets me on the mattress.

"There's nowhere I'd rather be than wherever you are," he says. I love him so much it hurts. My entire body aches.

"Agreed."

The next few days are, for lack of a better word, perfect. We use the boyfriend/girlfriend words, almost to excess. It becomes a running joke that only Javi and I find funny.

"I love knowing that you're mine," Javi says one night after we've had a particularly slow and sweet session of sex in front of the mirror. He's been talking about installing them on the ceiling and in panels on the walls, but I think that would be a little too much. I'd feel like I lived in a funhouse.

"Ditto. I like knowing that I'm the only one you're with." I'd wanted to claim him for ages.

"And I don't mean you're mine, like some sort of creepy possessive thing. I can't really explain it." I kiss the center of his chest where his tattoos converge and flare out.

"I know what you mean. You don't have to explain it. I know." I look up at him and he smiles.

"I know you know."

I know a lot of things about Javi now. I know that he mixes melted butter with his syrup and puts it on his waffles and pancakes, but won't put butter on the pancakes and then pour on the syrup. I know that he bites his bottom lip when he's working on a paper. I know that he believes in ghosts, humans and robots becoming one, and that music videos should still be on MTV.

I wonder what he now knows about me.

One night when I'm studying I hear him chuckle.

"What?"

"You're doing that thing. It's cute."

"What thing?" I have no idea what he's talking about.

He leans back and sets his book down.

"You mouth the words you type and sometimes you say them out loud." I give him a look. He's crazy. I do not do that.

"You're making that up."

He puts his arms up.

"It's true, I swear. I can video you to prove it." I narrow my eyes at him. I think I would know if I was doing something like that. And no one's ever said anything before.

"I think you're messing with me."

"Fine, fine." He picks up his book again and I go back to typing my paper. But I'm so self-conscious I can't focus again.

"Damn you. Now I'm so busy focusing on what I do when I type that I can't type." Javi laughs.

"Sorry, gorgeous. My fault. Just ignore me." Well, if that isn't impossible, I don't know what is.

It takes me a few minutes to get back into paper writing mode, but I do. I finish what I need to get done and save the document only to look up and find Javi holding up his phone at me.

"What the fuck, Javi?" He gets up and hands the phone to me. Ugh, he took a video of me. I hit Play and watch as I do exactly what he said I did.

Huh.

"That's so weird," I say as I watch myself muttering like a crazy person over my paper. It's a good thing I don't write papers in public, or else I might look like a psycho working on her manifesto.

"I think of it as interesting. And adorable." Right. Because muttering to yourself is the height of cuteness. Whatever floats your boat, I guess.

"Whatever. I'm going to start taking videos of all your weird little quirks and then we'll see who the adorable one is." I hold the phone out of his reach and he snatches at it. I can't win the battle for the phone, but I can definitely win another way.

I lean back on the couch and hold the phone as far away as it will go. Javi has to climb on top of me to grab it and I put my plan into action. I wrap my legs around him and grind a few times. He stops reaching for the phone and looks down at me.

"You're dirty," he says.

"Yup. Wanna clean me up?"

He shakes his head slowly.

"No. I want to get dirty with you." The phone drops from my hand, but he doesn't notice. I hope it isn't broken, but I'll get him a new one if it is.

"Oh? How dirty?"

He dips his head down and licks the spot under my ear that drives me crazy.

"Filthy," he says in my ear.

"Well, I think I'm going to need to see a demonstration."

He licks the spot again and gets off me before picking me up and taking me to the bedroom to show me just how incredibly filthy he can be.

I enjoy every disgusting second.

Chapter Twenty-One

"So, are you good with the whole girlfriend thing?" Shannon asks me as we sit down with our lattes at the café on campus. We've been spending more time with just the two of us lately, and I realize how much I've missed talking with just her. Maybe we should send the boys back to their place tonight and have a sleepover just the two of us.

"It's weird and not weird at the same time. Which doesn't make any sense," I say.

"No, it makes perfect sense. I totally get it." Shannon nods and I know she knows. "I thought when Jett and I started dating, you know, after we made it real and everything, that it was going to be different. It was and it wasn't."

"Exactly."

We share a smile.

"But it's good? You seem so happy," she says, taking a bite of her Danish.

"Yeah, it's really good. So good that I sometimes can't believe it's even happening, you know? It seems like a movie or a romance novel or something, and not real life."

"It feels that way." I sip my coffee and then Shannon says something I don't expect.

"So, I think I want to move in with Jett." I can tell she's been holding onto this and has wanted to tell me for a while.

"Oh, wow. Are you sure?" This is quite a change from what she said a few days ago.

"Yeah, I think I am. I just needed a few days to get used to the idea. You know, process. And the more I thought about it, the more I liked the idea. I mean, we're practically living together now anyway. But I didn't want to say anything to him until I'd talked to you about it. And I won't do it if you don't want me to. Or I can wait until the summer or whatever. It doesn't have to be right now, but I wanted to know what you thought. So, what do you think?" She keeps twisting her fingers together.

What do I think?

I have no idea.

"Well, I think it's great. You are practically living together so it makes sense. And things are crowded anyway. And his apartment is pretty shitty, so you could probably get a better place together." I say all the right things, but inside I feel like I want to cry and throw up at the same time.

If Shannon moves in with Jett, then I'll either have to find another roommate, or move in with Javi. And I am not ready for that.

I know how hypocritical I'm being, but I don't care. I can't help the way I feel about it. If Javi and I moved in together, then we'd be sharing the rent and what would happen if/when we break up? Then one of us would have to move out and I'd have to search for a new roommate anyway.

I could live with one of my friends, but I don't know if that would be a good idea. I'm not that easy to live with and I don't have a lot of patience with roommates. Shannon is the exception.

She lets out a breath.

"Good. I'm glad you feel that way. It would kill me if you got upset. Because I love Jett, but you're my best friend. I can't be happy if you're not happy." I have to look away from her so I don't start crying in the middle of the coffee place.

I really don't deserve her as a friend. And I can't tell her that I don't want her to move. She's so happy with Jett and I can't stand in the way of that.

"I love you too. And I want you to be happy and Jett makes you happy. I'll figure things out, don't you worry. I'm a big girl." Shannon beams and gets up from her chair. In the middle of the café she throws her arms around me.

"You're the best! Oh, could you not say anything to Jett about it? Or Javi? I want to figure some things out first before I talk to Jett. And I want to give you enough time to figure things out too." Right. Figure things out.

"I won't breathe a word," I say and she smacks a kiss on my cheek. I make a face and pretend to wipe it off.

I can't stop thinking about what Shannon and I talked about for the rest of the day. I get a sick feeling in the pit of my stomach whenever I remember what she said. I didn't care so much when moving was just a possibility, but now that it's a definite, I realize how much I hate the idea. Selfish as it may be, I don't want things to change. At least not right now, and not like this. If I was moving in with Javi, that would be one thing, but I didn't get to make the choice this time. It was made for me and I fucking hate it.

And the biggest downside is that I can't get my best friend's opinion on it, and I can't talk to Javi either. So I'm on my own to be miserable.

Javi notices the second I walk in the door. Shannon's still at work, so I don't have to completely put on a happy face for her. At least not yet.

"What's wrong, babe?" He looks up from a pot that's simmering something that smells absolutely amazing. Lately he's been talking about getting a crockpot so he can start cooking in the morning and let whatever it is simmer all day. I'm totally on board with this plan.

"Nothing," I say as I give him a hug and a kiss. "You know, we should really get you an apron." Briefly, I imagine Javi cooking in just an apron and nothing else. It's not a terrible image, so I make a note to get him one for his birthday next month.

"You sure? You have Hazel Sad Face." I give him a look.

"How is that different from my regular face?"

"It just is. So, tell me what's wrong."

I don't like how well he knows me and knows the expressions on my face. I'm going to have to get better at hiding my emotions if I want to have any success as a lawyer.

"It's nothing, really. I don't want to talk about it, please?" I duck out from under his arm and go to put my bag in the bedroom.

"Okay," Javi says when I come back.

"Thanks, babe."

If I'm bad at hiding my sad face, then Shannon would win an award for not being able to hide her happy one. She's beaming so hard when she walks through the door that I'm afraid she's going to break her face.

"Whoa, did someone have their happy pills this morning?" Javi asks.

"Nope." She shakes her head and bounces a little on her feet. "Just happy about things." Javi gives me a questioning look, but I just shrug.

"Well, whatever the reason for your happiness, I'm happy you're happy." He gives her a hug and she has to get up on her tiptoes to reciprocate.

"Thanks, Javi," she says and skips to her room.

Javi just shakes his head at her.

"She has got to be medicated. No one is that fucking happy. You know what's up?" I wish he hadn't asked me. I don't want to lie to him. I open my mouth to do it anyway and the words won't come. I just can't lie to Javi.

"I'll tell you, but you have to swear to me you'll keep your mouth shut and won't tell Jett. Or else I will dismember you in your sleep. Got it?" I can't believe I'm doing this. Shannon is going to kill me. I'm the worst friend ever.

"Former scout's honor," Javi says and crosses his heart. "I know how to keep my mouth shut, Haze." I bet he does. I motion for him to lean closer, just in case Shannon decides to come out of her room.

"She's decided to move in with Jett. I guess she finally thought about it and she wants to now."

"No shit, really?" Javi seems very excited about this news, which is a little weird. I guess he's just happy for her. "That's fucking great. I'm guessing she hasn't told him, which is why we're keeping this on the down low." I'm about to respond when Shannon comes back. I just nod.

"What's for dinner?" she asks as she looks into the pot. "I don't really care what it is because it smells amazing."

"It's going to be pulled pork sandwiches when it's done. Thought I'd go a little simple tonight." It sounds simple, but it won't be the way Javi makes it.

"I want to live in this pot," Shannon says and inhales the steam coming from the simmering meat and sauce.

"Like a pulled pork sauna," he says and they both laugh. I'm too busy thinking about the fact that I just betrayed my best friend to think about pork saunas. But I put on a smile and fake a quick laugh for the sake of saving face. The arrival of Jett distracts Shannon even more and by the way she's looking at him, I'm thinking she wants to dip him in the pork sauna and then devour him.

Javi grins at me and then winks. I smile back, but it makes my heart hurt. This is a no-win situation.

In an effort to get things out in the open, I corner Shannon that night while the guys are in the living room talking about… guy things.

"Hey, so, when are you going to tell Jett about the whole moving in thing? Have I said how happy I am for you and how I want you to be happy?" Whoa. Coming on a little too strong there. Gotta tone it down.

"Ummmm," she says, fiddling with some jewelry on her dresser. "I kind of already told him. Like a few minutes after I talked to you. I couldn't help it. I was just so excited." Oh. So Jett already knows. So it wasn't technically wrong for me to tell Javi. Even though I didn't know that Jett knew at the time I told Javi.

Ugh, this is getting complicated.

"And? What did he think?" Shannon beams again and grabs onto me.

"He said that he wants it, so it's happening!" She squeals and throws herself at me. "I know I said I didn't want it, but the more I thought about it, the more sense it made. And I love Jett. He loves me. That's all that matters, right?"

I nod and hug her back.

"You're not mad that I told him before you'd had time to think and figure everything out, are you?"

"No, no. You're excited, nothing wrong with that at all. I'm so happy for you. Where do you think you're going to go?" She's practically wiggling with excitement.

"Well, we want to get something a little bit nicer and maybe within walking distance of campus. Then Jett wouldn't have to drive that deathtrap so much. I worry about him every time he leaves in that thing." Jett's car is something else. I wouldn't ride in it if you paid me. That thing is an accident waiting to happen.

"That sounds really nice."

"I'm sorry to spring this on you. Are you going to be okay?" I'll be okay if she stops asking me if I'm going to be okay. Instead of snapping at her, I smile.

"Yeah, I'll be absolutely fine. No worries. I can take care of myself. Have for years." Shannon hugs me again and we go back out to the living room. Shannon takes Jett's hand and pulls him to his feet.

"We have an announcement. Jett and I are moving in together." Jett smiles down at Shannon and she smiles at him and they're so fucking happy I can barely stand it. They deserve happy, both of them.

"Well, that's great. Just great," Javi says, giving Jett one of those back-slapping guy hugs and he gives Shannon one that lifts her off her feet and he swings her around. I applaud and say how happy I am and all that.

"This calls for a celebration," Javi says, going to the kitchen. Something tells me it's not going to be champagne that he brings out.

I'm absolutely right. Javi has a bottle of whiskey under one arm and four brand new shot glasses.

"Now this is my kind of toasting," he says, setting down the glasses and unscrewing the top on the bottle before pouring us all generous shots.

Shannon and Jett grab theirs and I pick mine up as well. Javi raises his and we all follow suit.

"To Jett and Shannon and their new life together. May they be blessed with happiness, laughter and lots of fucking." I snort, and raise my glass before tipping it back and letting the alcohol burn its way down my throat. Shannon has to take hers in two gulps, but she gets it down and wipes her mouth.

"Nice toast, Javi. Very classy," she says.

"Well, I'll have an even better one for your wedding." I stare at him. "What?"

"Um, isn't it a little too early to be talking about that? And what do you care? Do you have a wedding fetish that I don't know about?" This is all new information to me.

Javi does the one-shoulder-shrug.

"No, I just figure when Jett and Shannon get married, I'll be the best man. What's crazy about that?" Well, when you put it that way, it doesn't sound crazy at all.

"Forget I said anything. I'm just tired," I say and set my shot glass back on the table. I don't want to talk about weddings or moving in or any of that stuff.

"Whoa, I swear I'm drunk already," Shannon says, laughing.

Javi just grins and pours another shot.

"You in?" he asks me.

"Sure."

"Me too," Jett says, but Shannon shakes her head. The three of us do another shot. I'm definitely going to be feeling this in the morning, but I don't care about that. All I care about is right now and trying to think or feel something other than shitty.

"I think that should be it for me," Jett says, turning down Javi for a third shot.

"I'll do another if we wait a few minutes," I say.

"Fair enough."

Instead of watching a movie like we usually do, Shannon brings out a deck of cards and we play Go Fish. I honestly can't remember the last time I played, but it was a long time ago. It's much more fun when you're somewhat drunk.

Jett and Shannon turn in early, probably due to the effects of the alcohol, but Javi and I stay up.

"What about that third shot?" I nod and he pours it for me. It's too quiet so I put on some music. Normally I don't listen to anything that's modern, but Shannon's been playing this guy Hozier a lot lately and I really like his stuff. "In a Week" starts to softly play as I sit on the couch again with Javi and he hands me my shot.

We both down ours without toasting this time.

"I did something you're probably going to be really angry about," Javi says, setting his glass down. "I needed to be drunk to tell you."

Chapter Twenty-Two

"Tell me what?"

"Before you get mad," he says, completely ignoring my question, "I didn't plan this. It just happened." Oh, shit. I want to throw up. I don't even know what he did, but obviously it's something bad. I knew it. We were too good to be true. It's over.

"What did you do, Javi?" I say, my voice soft. I'm raging inside, but I can't bring myself to yell.

Javi looks down at his hands and then up at me.

"I bought a house."

Of all the things I thought he was going to say, that was not it. I expected him to tell me that he cheated on me, or... well, that was pretty much what I assumed he was going to say. But a house? I think I need to hear him say it again so I can make sure I heard him right.

"A house? What do you mean a house?"

"I bought a house. Well, it's more like a duplex, actually. I saw it and it was for sale and I went in and the next thing I knew I was signing the paperwork. It's Jett's fault, really. He was the one who asked Shannon to move in and then I got the idea in my head." He gets up and starts pacing around the room and it's like he's possessed.

"It's crazy, right? Who does that? I don't even know why I bought it, but I did. I bought a house. I bought a house."

I'm still on the couch and I can't seem to form a response. This is just… I don't know what to say.

"Mimi and I always lived in apartments. Never a house. She always wanted a house with enough space so she could have an herb garden. She used to grow little pots of basil and thyme and rosemary in the windows of our apartment, but they never got much sun. I always told her I'd use my money to buy her a house where she could have a garden." His voice is softer now.

"Who did you buy the house for, Javi?" I ask. I want to hear his answer.

"Well, I bought it for me, and for you. And for Jett and Shannon, if they want to move in with us. I thought… I figured you wouldn't want things to change too much, and if they didn't, then you'd be less reluctant to move in with me." I can't process this.

"But, Javi. We've barely started dating. I just… this is too much too fast. What happens if we break up? Then what? Then where do I live? Huh? Where do I live? I can't live with Shannon because she's moving in with Jett and I can't live with other people because I hate everyone else and I can't afford a place of my own." I can feel myself losing it, but I've been holding this back for a while now and it's finally coming out.

"We're already living together, Haze. Our location won't change that." I rub my eyes to stop the tears from flowing, but they won't.

"But it will. It will be different. You know it will. I just… I can't deal with this right now." I get up and head for the kitchen. I have a secret stash of cigarettes on the highest shelf of one of the cabinets. I figured Shannon would never discover it since she's so short. I grab the pack and a lighter and go outside.

Javi follows me. I light up and inhale. Oh, I needed that. I also definitely need another shot. What a fucked up day.

"Those things will kill you, you know," Javi says as I lean against the porch railing and watch the smoke curl into the sky and mingle with the stars.

"Something will. Might as well go out happy." I flick some ash and then hold the pack out to him. He takes one and uses a lighter from his pocket.

"I didn't mean to throw this on you. I really had a better plan. I was going to take you out to dinner and then drive you to the house and have it all set up with candles and everything. I was going to do this the right way, but I guess I got excited. You don't have to say anything, or make any decisions. The last thing I want you to do is feel forced to do something you don't want."

I exhale and try to put into words why I'm freaking out so much.

"My family was never there for me, growing up. The one group of people you're supposed to count on, and they weren't reliable. So I guess I just have a lot of trust issues." That's putting it lightly.

"What about Shannon?"

I shrug.

"She's different. I just... I trusted her the first time we met. I can't explain it. She's a good person, Javi. Such a good person. She's always worried about everyone else."

He leans closer to me.

"And what about me? Do you trust me?"

That's a more complicated answer.

"I want to. I do. But you have the power to break my heart. I gave you that power, but still. You scare me. The way I feel about you scares me."

Javi chuckles softly.

"Well, that's something we can definitely agree on. You scare the shit out of me. I always thought guys who were obsessed with their girlfriends were just whipped or getting some or whatever. But you... how I feel about you is something so... big. It's big and deep and feels endless. I can't imagine a day when I won't be in love with you. I don't want to imagine a world where that would happen." I ache at his words. I always wanted someone to say something like that to me, but never thought it would happen.

"I love you too. But I'm scared. That doesn't mean I don't want to be with you. To move in someday. But I guess I just need to move slower with that stuff."

Javi nods and finishes his cigarette.

"I can do that. Just... talk to me. I can't know how your head is working if you don't tell me." That's fair.

"Sure." We stub out our cigarettes, but I'm not ready to go inside yet. The air is warmer than it's been in a while.

"Are you going to tell Jett and Shannon about it?" I ask.

Javi shrugs.

"I don't know. I mean, I'm not even sure how that would work. They probably wouldn't just want to live there rent-free, so we'd have to figure that out. I told you, I really didn't plan this thing. It just happened."

"Well, of all the things that 'just happen' I'm glad it involved a house and not another girl's vagina." He throws back his head and laughs and dog at our neighbor's house barks at the noise.

"Did you think that was what I was going to tell you? That I fucked another girl?" I give him a look.

"Well, when your boyfriend says he's got something to tell you, it's not crazy to go there."

"Fair enough."

I move closer to him and he puts his arms around me. I inhale his smell and it's true. Javi feels like home. He feels like comfort and safety and all the things I've been searching for and craving my entire life.

I'm just so scared that it's going to be taken away from me.

"I'm never going to abandon you, Haze. Never, ever. I'd marry you right now to show you that." I stiffen. Is he serious?

I pull back and look at him.

Yup. He's fucking serious.

"You'd marry me, right here. Right now. On this porch. Better and worse, all of that. Right now." He nods once and then takes my face in both of his hands.

"I, Javier, take you, Hazel, to be my lawfully wedded wife. To have and to hold, in sickness and in health, for richer or poorer, from now until… forever." I can't move. I can't speak. I can't breathe.

"Your turn," he whispers and I reach up and hold his face. His cheeks have a little bit of stubble on them.

"I, Hazel, take you, Javier, to be my lawfully wedded husband." These words don't feel strange. They feel right and true and completely perfect.

"To have and to hold, in sickness and in health, for richer or poorer, from now until forever." Javi smiles slowly.

"See? Now that wasn't so bad, was it? I now pronounce us husband and wife. I may kiss my bride." He pulls me close for a kiss. Tears are coursing down my cheeks and my heart feels like it's going to beat its way out of my chest.

"I love you so much," Javi says as he breaks the kiss. His own eyes are a little shiny.

"I love you. I can't… I can't believe we just did that."

"Next time we should probably do it in front of people. And all legal and everything."

"Be serious, Javi."

"I am completely and totally serious. If you told me right this second you wanted to go to Vegas and do this, I'd be booking plane tickets." He is serious.

"This is crazy," I say. Absolutely crazy. I'm standing in front of a guy that I just "married" who has also bought a house for us to live in.

"I prefer to think of it as knowing what's right and going for it. You and I are right. I know it. Took me a little while to realize, but now that I do, I know I'd do anything to keep this. Anything."

"I'm not ready to get married, Javi. I'm not ready to move into your house." God, I don't want to hurt him. "But when I'm ready, you'll be the first to know."

"I should hope so, porch wife." That makes me laugh.

"So is that what I'm going to call you now? My porch husband?"

"I like that better than boyfriend, actually."

We kiss again and Javi starts swaying us back and forth.

"We should dance now, you know. The couple always does that at their wedding reception," he says and we start turning. There isn't much room since it's a small porch, but we can still dance a little.

"You know, we've both consumed alcohol and this entire thing could be blamed on the whiskey," I say and Javi makes a face.

"No way. I'm not even drunk."

"I'm getting there."

We sway some more and I start laughing.

"What's so funny?"

"This. You. Me. Everything."

"Funny isn't the word I would use," he says, taking my hand and twirling me under his arm.

"What word would you use?" I ask and then squeal as he dips me, being sure I don't hit my head on the porch railing.

"I'd use two words. Fucking perfect." I roll my eyes as he pulls me upright.

"Of course you'd use the word 'fucking'."

"Hey, it's one of my favorite words to use and activities to participate in." Heat flares between us and I can see some in our near future.

"You're fucking ridiculous, porch husband."

"You're fucking awesome, porch wife."

Chapter Twenty-Three

I don't tell Shannon about Javi's and my porch marriage. It's one of those things I don't want to tell anyone. I want to keep that special moment just to myself. And Javi, of course.

I only call him my porch husband when we're alone, but he calls me porch wife the next night at dinner.

"What are you talking about?" Shannon asks. I glare at Javi.

"Oh, it's a long story. I was a little drunk. It doesn't even make sense now." I smile at him and he smiles back.

"No, it doesn't make a whole lot of sense."

Javi shrugs one shoulder.

"I was drunk."

Over the next week, Shannon and Jett start looking for apartments. The search doesn't go well. It's an odd time of year to start looking, since most students won't be moving out until after finals or during the summer.

"Well, I swear I saw a rat at that last place, so that's out," Shannon says as she crosses out the apartment listings from the paper. She's also been looking online, but those listings can be questionable.

"Ugh, why is this so hard? We just want a one-bedroom. I mean, we'd take a loft. A freaking loft!" She throws up her hands.

"Well, you don't have to find anything right this minute. Maybe if you wait you'll find something." I've also been asking around to see if anyone knows of a place, but zip. There are plenty of disgusting shitholes, but that's not what Shannon and Jett are looking for.

I haven't told her about the house and Javi hasn't told Jett. I have no idea what the place even looks like. I've thought about asking Javi to take me there, but I still need more time. I feel kind of awful that Shannon and Jett going through all this to find a place when Javi has a place that they could live in if they wanted.

We talk about it in bed.

"I think you should at least tell them. Give them the option. Because they're finding nothing right now. And… I'd like knowing they were in a place that you're running. At least they won't have a shitty landlord who will screw them over."

I'm not going to do anything about my housing situation until Shannon has a definite plan.

"Are you sure? I was looking at rents for different places and I think I figured out a rate. The place needs a few repairs first and so forth and I need to get a renter's agreement together and do some other paperwork, but I think this could work really well. And then I can spend my time convincing you to move into the other unit. It's got a really great kitchen. And I may have ordered a Jacuzzi tub." He wiggles his eyebrows and I jab him in the chest with my finger.

"You are not going to bribe me to move in with you by getting me a tub, porch husband." He rubs the spot I poked, as if I'd hurt him.

"That's not going to stop me from trying, porch wife."

The next day Shannon attacks me as soon as I walk through the door.

"Did you know that Javi bought a house?" Guess he told her.

"Yes. He told me that night you and Jett announced you were moving in. I'd blame it on the whiskey, but I don't think that was it. I still don't really know why he did it, but he did. So. There you have it. Kind of a perfect solution, when you think about it."

"And you can honestly tell me you're okay with this?" I shrug.

"I'm getting more okay. I wasn't at first, that's for sure. And I haven't agreed to move in with him." It seems a moot point. Kind of inevitable now.

"Where the hell did he get the money for a house?" I hadn't anticipated that question. I don't know what Javi wants me to say. "I mean, I know he said he has some sort of inheritance that he's been holding onto, but that's just too weird."

I don't want to give anything away about Javi's past and family. It's up to him if he wants to share that with her.

"Has Jett told you anything about Javi's past?"

She shakes her head.

"Nope. I've asked, but he's a vault. Which is kind of sweet in a way. I love their relationship." So do I. It's my favorite bromance.

"Oh. Well. I've also got it in the vault. But you might want to ask him." I have a feeling Javi would trust Shannon with this. She's much more trustworthy than I am.

"Maybe I will. I'm definitely interested. But back to the house." That damn house.

I'm starting to resent the house now. It's all anyone can talk about at dinner.

"So, how big are we talking?" Shannon asks. She wants to know each and every minute detail of the place while Jett just wants to argue with Javi about how much rent to pay. And I'm sitting there and wishing I could go somewhere else.

"Well, I think it's definitely something to consider," Shannon says. "Could we maybe see the place this weekend?"

"Yeah, sure. There's some renovations going on, but you can get the idea. You want to come?" The last part is directed at me.

"I don't know. Maybe." I really don't want to. Part of the reason is that I don't want to get pushed into this moving-in thing and the other part is that I'm afraid I'm going to fall in love with the place. And then what? I'd have no reason not to do it.

"I think you'd really like it," he says. Javi has not stopped his campaign to convince me to move in so I know a lot about the house already. It's like he knows exactly what I'd want in a house and has decided to tease me with it. He's getting really good at it, which is driving me nuts.

"We'll see," I say. I'm still on the fence.

"Come, porch wife. I swear you won't regret it." Oh, I might.

"Okay, okay," I say. "I'll go."

Javi beams at me and I know I'm probably going to regret this.

Javi is so excited when we wake up on Saturday morning. Like, beyond excited. I've never seen him that excited. Not even at the prospect of sex.

"You ready?" he asks as I put my hair up in the mirror. I'm trying to move as slow as I can. Jett and Shannon are already waiting in the living room. Jett's started folding cranes out of notebook paper and lining them up on the coffee table.

"I guess," I say, smoothing the sides of my hair even though they won't be smoothed. The plague of having curly hair.

"Come on, it'll be fun. Promise, porch wife." He holds out his arms and I walk into them.

"You'd better be right, porch husband."

We gather up Jett and Shannon and head out to my car, since it's the most reliable vehicle that will fit four people in it, but Javi has to drive since I don't know where the place is.

We head closer to campus and then turn down a little side street I've never noticed before. It's so close to school that I can see the football stadium through the trees. Javi drives down a street, flanked by very suburban and nice family houses on either side.

I almost gasp when he pulls into the driveway of a duplex. It's a nice tan color with white trim and is basically two cute houses connected by an entryway. There's a front yard with a brick path leading up to each door and there's a garage attached to either side of the house.

"Here we are," Javi says, driving up to one of the garages that's part of the house on the left side.

"This is it? Javi, this is beautiful," Shannon says, staring openmouthed at the houses. It's... it's more than beautiful. It's spectacular.

"Come on," Javi says, getting out and walking toward the front door. It takes me a few seconds to make my legs work to get out of the car and follow him. Jett and Shannon are behind me and they're whispering to each other.

"So, this is your unit and then the other unit is… unoccupied at the moment." Everyone looks at me and I really wish I hadn't come. This was a bad idea.

Javi unlocks the door and we walk in. I almost gasp again.

"Oh, wow," Shannon says. I can't say anything.

Javi takes my hand.

"So, this is the foyer, obviously, and here's the living room and kitchen." The first floor has an open plan, with the living room and kitchen only separated by an island and off to the side is an area that could be a formal dining room. A set of glass doors leads out to a porch in the back and the yard.

"What do you think?" Jett and Shannon have identical bug-eyed expressions on their faces. I probably look the same.

"It's just… wow, Javi."

"Seriously, man. This is something else," Jett says. Javi squeezes my hand.

"Why don't you guys head upstairs and check out the bedrooms and bathrooms." It doesn't escape my notice that he said bedrooms, plural. Jett and Shannon head up the stairs, still talking, and I'm left downstairs with Javi.

"What do you think?" he asks me.

"I don't know what to say, honestly. This is… this is too much Javi. Way too much. I didn't think it was going to be a whole house. You said duplex and apartment and I thought… this is a house. Two houses. With garages and yards and shit. What the hell were you thinking?" I'm trying to keep my voice down, but it's not easy.

"But what do you think about it?" He's completely ignored what I just said. "Put all that aside and look at the actual house. What do you think?"

"It's nice," I say and let go of his hand. It's much more than nice. I don't even need to see the upstairs to know it's beautiful. I always wanted to live in a house like this. A house that has an actual dining room and a fireplace and a backyard that isn't full of trash and car parts. A house that doesn't have a fridge full of beer and old pizza. A house that would be decorated for holidays. A house full of pictures and memories, more good than bad.

This is what I've always wanted.

The tears start again and I turn away from Javi to hide them.

"Haze?"

I shake my head and walk toward the kitchen. The counters are out-of-date, but I don't care. They're much nicer than anything I've ever lived with.

"If you hate it, you can tell me. You're not going to hurt my feelings." I shake my head again.

"I don't hate it. It's beautiful. It's perfect. How could I not love it?" I turn back to him and he sees the tears. Immediately, he comes to me and holds me, rocking me back and forth and rubbing my back.

"You've got to tell me what's going on in your head."

"I know. This is just a lot for me. When I was growing up, all I wanted was a house like this. I dreamed about it. I asked Santa for a house like this every year. Even after I didn't believe in Santa. I used to pray to Jesus during my brief foray into Christianity. I wished and hoped for it, but I never thought it would happen. Not really. And here you are, and I'm in love with you, which I also never thought would happen, and now you're handing me a dream house and it's just too good to be true." There it is. This is too good to be true. My life just can't be tied up this easily. Perfect guy, perfect house.

"Oh, Haze. I had no idea about the house. Why didn't you tell me?" I bury my head in his chest and close my eyes.

"I don't know. I didn't want to talk about it."

"I understand. I think that's why I bought this place. Because I always wanted a house too." That's right. I've been thinking totally and completely about myself and haven't even given Javi a thought.

"I'm so sorry. I'm being selfish and mean and I'm sorry. You've done this amazing thing and I'm being totally ungrateful and awful. How do you put up with me?" I really do wonder.

"Because I love you, porch wife. It isn't any more complicated than that. I love you and I want to be with you and have a home with you. Because when I'm with you I feel like I'm home and I want to have that all the time." He makes everything sound so simple. I just get wrapped up in my stupid head and get all pessimistic about everything. To be fair, not a whole lot has worked out for me thus far in life, so my expectations are of failure. And then I met Shannon and then I met Javi and everything changed. Now my life seems like a dream. That sounds corny, but it's true.

"I love you. And I love the house. And I love being with you and I want to have a home with you. I want to come home from class and find you cooking in our kitchen. I want to go to bed with you and wake up with you in our bed. Maybe we could get a cat?" I always wanted a cat. The closest I ever got was when I fed this mean-as-hell stray that lived in one of the trailer parks I grew up in.

Javi nodded and kissed both of my cheeks.

"Yes, we can get a cat."

Chapter Twenty-Four

Shannon and Jett come downstairs and proclaim their love for the place. Then Javi and I go upstairs and check everything out. There are two bedrooms and two bathrooms and an extra room that could be an office. If I could make a blueprint of my perfect house, this would be it. I don't even need to see the other house since it's a mirror image of this one.

We all congregate again and I can tell Shannon is bursting.

"We'll do it!" She throws herself at Javi and starts to cry and Jett is hugging him and banging him on the back and my eyes are getting wet again.

"This is just so wonderful, Javi, I can't even begin to think about how we're going to thank you." He tries to wave them off.

"Really, it's not a big deal. I'm just glad it worked out so well. Didn't plan it that way." I look at Javi and he puts his arm around me.

The four of us stand in Jett and Shannon's new living room in silence. Like none of us can believe where we are. Then Shannon starts laughing.

"This is insane. I keep waiting for cameras to come around the corner and tell me this is all some sort of joke, or new reality show. I know that's not going to happen, but…" Yeah, I know.

"We're going to get a cat. What about you guys?" Javi says, squeezing my shoulder.

"Wait, does that mean you're going to be moving in too?" Shannon says, looking back and forth from me to Javi.

I look up at him and give him a kiss.

"Yeah. We're moving in." Then there's another round of hugging and crying and jumping around. Shannon and I are responsible for most of it.

I was so reluctant to agree to this, but now that I have… it feels so right. So right. And good. And perfect.

"Okay, close your eyes," Javi says as we get out of the car and he leads me up the walkway to our new house. We haven't moved in yet, but we will as soon as some of the renovations are done.

I close my eyes and Javi leads me through the front door. We walk a few steps and then he makes me stop.

"Open," he says in my ear and I open my eyes.

The room is flooded with candlelight. There must be hundreds of candles in here. I wonder where he got them all. They cover almost every surface, including the folding table he's set up in the dining room. We haven't had a chance to pick out furniture yet.

"Oh, Javi." He kisses the side of my head and leads me to the table and pulls out a folding chair for me.

"I know it's not ideal, but I figured the candles would help with the atmosphere. And I did say I'd foot the bill for two dinners if I lost the bet, so." He shrugs one shoulder and then goes to the stove and dishes something out and brings the plates over. There are plastic cups and wine and it's not perfect, which makes it totally perfect.

We clink our plastic cups and I pick up my plastic fork to start working on the eggplant parmesan Javi has made, but he gets up.

"I just have one more thing to show you." He goes upstairs and comes back down carrying something.

He holds it out and presents it to me.

"I didn't want her running around with the candles everywhere."

Inside the pet carrier is a sweet little kitten.

"Oh my God, Javi."

"You said you wanted a cat. I found her at the humane society and I couldn't leave her there." He opens the carrier and takes the kitten out and sets her in my lap. She's white and black and orange, with patches all over her. Calico, I think they call it. She meows and looks up at me and I can't even breathe.

"See? Now how could you resist that face?" Javi leans down and strokes the top of her head and she leans into his hand and starts purring.

"She's so cute. I love her." I mean, what's not to love?

"Good. We should probably put her back in the carrier until we're done with the candles." Javi gently places her back in the carrier and sets it on the floor. She cries and the sound almost breaks my heart. Javi and I share a look before we both start blowing out the candles.

"Where the hell did you get all these candles, anyway?" I ask.

"Couple of places. I also ordered some online and had them shipped overnight. It's a good thing we have a basement or else I wouldn't have a place to put them." True.

Once we get all the candles put out, I sit on the floor and open the carrier. The kitten marches out and sniffs around and then comes right for me. Javi sits down next to me and she goes to him and climbs in his lap.

"Great. It looks like I have some competition." Javi strokes her head and she starts purring like crazy.

"Yeah, you might. But can you blame me?" The kitten yawns and it's so adorable I can't even stand it.

"Not really. What are we going to call her?"

Javi shifts a little and the kitten protests.

"I don't know. I figured we could find a name when we'd gotten to know her a little. I always think it's weird when people name their kids before they're born. What if the kid comes out and the name doesn't work?"

"True. I never really thought of myself as a Hazel, but I've never thought about what I'd change it to if I did. But you're such a Javier."

He gives me a weird look.

"I am?"

I roll my eyes.

"Yeah, you are."

"Okay. Sure." He has no idea what I'm talking about, and that's fine.

"How about Mimi?" I suggest.

Javi looks down at the kitten. She looks right up at him. There's a black patch on her chin.

"Mimi." The kitten meows and I think that's a ringing endorsement.

"Yeah, Mimi," I say and pet her head.

"That's a good name."

"It is."

Acknowledgements

It took me a long time to write this book, and I have no idea why. Maybe I was worried I couldn't do Javi and Hazel's story justice. I don't know. But once I started, everything just flowed. I fell in love with Javi again and I had a great time writing their story. I hope you had as good a time reading it, or even better. Thanks go to my fabulous editor, Jen, my spectacular cover designer, Sarah Hansen, who came up with the butterfly for the cover that completely inspired me and tied everything in the story together, my publicist Jessica from InkSlinger PR, who, even thought she is expecting, still manages to work so hard for her authors. I debated a lot about writing this story, and I finally decided to do it for YOU. Yes, YOU. I had so many people come to me at signings, and sending me messages about how much you loved the first book. I couldn't ignore those. So thank you for your enthusiasm. Without it, this story might not have gotten told.

About the Author

Chelsea M. Cameron is a YA/NA and Adult New York Times/USA Today Best Selling author from Maine. Lover of things random and ridiculous, Jane Austen/Charlotte and Emily Bronte Fangirl, red velvet cake enthusiast, obsessive tea drinker, vegetarian, former cheerleader and world's worst video gamer. When not writing, she enjoys watching infomercials, singing in the car and tweeting. She has a degree in journalism from the University of Maine, Orono that she promptly abandoned to write about the people in her own head. More often than not, these people turn out to be just as weird as she is.

Find Chelsea online:

chelseamcameron.com

Twitter: @chel_c_cam

Facebook: Chelsea M. Cameron (Official Author Page)

Other Books by Chelsea M. Cameron

The Noctalis Chronicles
Nocturnal (Book One)
Nightmare (Book Two)
Neither (Book Three)
Neverend (Book Four)

The Whisper Trilogy
Whisper (Book One)

Rise and Fall
Deeper We Fall (Book One)
Faster We Burn (Book Two)

My Favorite Mistake (Available from Harlequin)
My Sweetest Escape (Available from Harlequin)

The Surrendering Saga
Sweet Surrendering (Book One)
Surrendering to Us (Book Two)
Coming Soon:
Dark Surrendering (Book Three)

Deep Surrendering

Rules of Love
For Real (Book One)

UnWritten

CPSIA information can be obtained
at www.ICGtesting.com
Printed in the USA
LVHW021653190319
611166LV00015B/319/P

9 781503 129283